Broken Sky

Part Five

Broken Sky

Part Five

Chris Wooding

Cover and illustrations by Steve Kyte

SCHOLASTIC

Scholastic Children's Books,
Commonwealth House, 1-19 New Oxford Street,
London WC1A 1NU, UK
a division of Scholastic Ltd
London ~ New York ~ Toronto ~ Sydney ~ Auckland
Mexico City ~ New Delhi ~ Hong Kong

First published in the UK by Scholastic Ltd, 2000

Text copyright © Chris Wooding, 2000
Illustrations copyright © Steve Kyte, 2000

ISBN 0 439 01491 3

Typeset by M Rules
Printed by Bath Press, England

10 9 8 7 6 5 4 3 2 1

Check out the

Broken Sky

website

www.homestead.com/gar_jenna

1

The Central Pivot

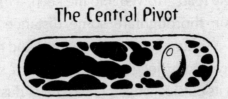

The keep of Takami-kos, Thane of Maar, stood alone in the midst of a grassy expanse of land, far removed from the nearest of the farming hamlets and towns that dotted the province. It was shaped like a snowflake, with its six symmetrical arms radiating outward from the central section. The arms were fat and rounded at the ends, displaying the usual Kirin disdain for corners, crafted of many huge bands of dull green metal pocked with high windows of Dominion glass. From the central section, a stubby tower thrust upwards, widening and then tapering at the top. It had none of the high spires of the Princess's palace, Fane Aracq; instead it was low and flat, hugging the ground jealously. And yet for all that, it could be seen for many miles around, across the level and

1

unwrinkled farmland of Maar: an elegant green starfish, dim in the twilight.

A single road arrowed into the keep, a tributary of a main thoroughfare some distance away. Along it, a solitary land-train steamed and roared, its massive body jogging up and down slightly between its outsize wheels, a vast fin of dust rising from the trail behind it, silver beneath the Kirin Taq sun. A great hiss of pistons and brakes came from it as it began to decelerate, closing in on its destination. In the central section of the keep, between two of the stubby metal arms, a thick gate was clanking open to receive the new arrival. The land-train slowed further as it approached, until it was barely crawling by the time it slipped into the belly of the keep, and the gate clattered shut behind it.

No sooner had the great metal creature settled in a slowly dispersing skirt of its own steam than the workers in the vehicle bay began to attend to it. The land-train was late, and it was near the end of their shift, and they wanted to get the job done before the new batch of workers came on, or the unloading orders would get confused and heads would roll. Hurried eyes glanced at their Glimmer shards as they went about their work, scampering up and down the ramp that had lowered from the land-train's underbelly. Kirins ran this way and that while the maintenance crew set to work on checking over the metal body of the machine. The crew's green uniforms, stained with oil, were supplemented by thick wyvern-hide gloves and heavy masks of the same, with protective bibs that covered their upper chest and back. Occasionally, the land-train would emit a scalding jet of steam across them as they worked; but encased in their armour, they were safe, and simply wiped the condensation off their round lenses and carried on.

In all the chaos, nobody noticed two of the maintenance crew walking away from the vehicle. They *looked* like they knew what they were doing, and they strode confidently in the manner of those who were supposed to be where they were. Anonymous behind their masks, they crossed the vehicle bay and slipped away unseen, leaving the noise and hustle behind them.

They halted in a dirty antechamber, caked with

grime, with dark pipes rumbling menacingly along the walls. Plain chests of wood were pushed up against the corners of the room, most lying open to reveal the clothes within. Some were the uniforms of the workers and maintenance crew; others were the simple, day-to-day clothes of the Maar people.

"Let's get before the next shift turns up," Whist said, pulling off his mask and shaking his multicoloured hair out. A moment later, Blink winked into existence next to him. They had been forced to leave him in the land-train while they crossed the vehicle bay, as the dog would draw too much attention; but now, seeing through Whist's eyes, Blink could confidently make the jump to his master's side. Ryushi looked at him warily. He'd had enough of that winking trick to last him a long time.

The journey across the province had been uncomfortable, but it could have been much worse. Once inside the vast cargo bay of the land-train, the stowaways had secreted themselves in the darkest corner that they could find and concealed themselves until the loading-ramp had been closed, plunging them into pitch darkness. Whist had thoughtfully brought a glowstone with him, stolen from the very keep that they were heading for, so they stretched and walked around between the tied-down stacks of crates and sacks. Whist assured him that there was no way into the cargo hold except via the loading ramp, and they would feel the land-train slowing to a stop long before anyone could open that. Once they had tired of investigating their surroundings, Whist entertained himself by telling Ryushi stories of his exploits on Os Dakar and what he had done in the year since his escape. Ryushi suspected most of what he said to be lies, but he was content to listen to pass the time, sitting cross-legged in the sickly orange light of the glowstone.

Whist was interrupted by the land-train's brakes beginning to grip, and the slight lurch as they began to decelerate.

Ryushi had known there would be some kind of checks carried out on the vehicle. Despite the difficulty of getting on to a land-train in the first place, he knew Takami wouldn't let any kind of transport inside the walls of his palace without it being thoroughly searched first. Whist had agreed with him, but told him not to worry; it was all in hand.

"They do a check at the last depot before the palace," he said, unhurriedly leading Ryushi back to their hiding-place with the loping, orange-tinged shadow of Blink at his heels. "Course, it helps if you know the routine. They check the outside first, then post guards on the exits and do the interior. That way, nothing gets out and slips past them." He ruffled the short, coarse hair on Blink's neck. "'Less you have a Flicker Dog with you."

In this way, they managed to evade the guards that combed the land-train. After waiting for the clanking of the exterior check to subside, they watched as the loading-ramp was opened in a cloud of steam, bringing a dim, grimy light from the depot into their hiding place. Holding on to Blink, they winked out of the cargo hold and took shelter in the shadow of one of the huge wheels of the land-train. The guards had lost interest in the vehicle now that they had scoured the metal skin for stowaways, and had taken up posts facing outwards, watching for any intruders in the depot.

Well-hidden in the darkness, the three interlopers stayed patient and motionless until the guards that were searching the interior left by the ramp, and the sentries that watched over it dispersed. The ramp closed, they winked back into the cargo hold, and so the check was passed.

Ryushi didn't trust Whist, didn't even like him. But he had to respect him. The boy was good; him and that dog of his.

Now, in the antechamber, they stripped off their protective suits and uniforms and stashed them away in a chest. It had been their good fortune that the land-train had been bringing a new consignment of gear for the depot workers, lashed together in hemp sacks. Ryushi thought it was perhaps a little *too* convenient, though. Maybe he wasn't giving them enough credit for their stealth so far, but he still could not shake the unwavering certainty that this was a trap, and that he was being allowed into Takami's keep with just enough obstacles to make the whole thing look realistic.

Maybe I'm paranoid, he thought. He glanced at Whist. *Probably not.*

It didn't matter. His honour forced his hand to vengeance, no matter what the risk to himself. His father's spirit demanded it.

"Nobody wears these things outside of the depot," Whist informed him, pulling off his wyvern-hide gloves, which he had slipped on over his own metal one. "We'll do better just trying to get by unseen. If we're spotted, don't worry; the keep folk know me and Blink, and as long as they don't recognize you, there'll be no problem. Not that they ought to; I mean, most of them have never laid eyes on you before. And there's plenty of Dominion-folk around the keep, which Aurin lets your brother—"

Ryushi looked up sharply. Whist coughed.

"– lets *Takami* have around," he continued. "So our skin thing shouldn't be an issue. Shall we just go, huh?"

They crept out of the antechamber into the corridors of the keep. There were few people out and about; the Glimmer shards that were occasionally set into a wall-bracket shone faintly blue in the light of the torches, and Whist informed Ryushi that Takami's court was usually in session at this kind of time. That meant that most people were in the upper levels of the central section, a few floors above them. The arms of the keep were living quarters and kitchens, armouries and so on; that was where they wanted to go.

"Takami's bedchamber," Whist said. "You'll never get him alone anywhere else. You can bolt the door from inside, and by the time anyone gets to him he'll be dead, and we can escape with Blink." He grinned, talking quietly. "It'll be like he was killed by a ghost."

"No," Ryushi said. "I want everyone to know who killed him."

"Okay, okay, it's your show," Whist said. "Just remember what I get when it's through."

"We'll talk about that afterwards," Ryushi replied, mentally adding: *if I'm still alive by then.*

For a moment, he thought about refusing to go along with Whist's idea. If Whist *was* setting a trap, it was best to be as unpredictable as possible, so as to lessen any chance of walking directly into the loop of the snare. But Whist had unwittingly hit on exactly the plan that Ryushi had been formulating during the journey across Maar; and really, Ryushi didn't have any other alternatives that he could see working.

Are you really gonna trust this guy? a voice in his head queried in disbelief.

I've got my stones, he thought to himself. *I'll be alright. Whist's got nothing he can pull on me that I can't handle with these.*

Maybe not Whist, but what about Takami? Or the Jachyra? continued his argumentative other.

I've beaten them both before, he replied. *I have to take the chance. No matter how much he's shown himself to be a liar in the past, I have to take the chance that he's telling the truth. It's the only way I can make Takami pay.*

They passed through the corridors of Takami's keep, trying to keep out of sight, avoiding contact with other people as much as possible. Sometimes they were able to hide as the sound of approaching footsteps warned them of danger; more often, they found themselves in a blank corridor with nowhere to turn as other keep-folk walked by them, and were forced to keep going and trust to luck. Each time, Ryushi felt his heart suddenly begin to thump in his ears; but he was not recognized, and some of them even nodded at Whist in a friendly fashion.

The interior of the place was more opulent than the smooth, metal exterior. It was decorated in shades of primarily dark green, white and blue. Ornaments were placed on window-sills, and crystalline plants stood in pots and beds against the walls. The theme of the keep seemed to revolve around a form of oddly kinked ceramic tile, which were placed in such a way that they overlapped each other like scales; and these, in various colours, were in evidence in almost every room and corridor, on sloping roofs, fountains and sills, lending contrast to the white stone of the interior walls. The now-familiar Kirin adherence to smooth lines was in effect once again, and as they progressed further from the central section towards the living quarters, the dwindling amount of people they saw allowed Ryushi time grudgingly to admire what his brother's treachery had brought him.

Then they passed into a wide chamber, and all thoughts of admiration went sour in his belly.

It was a mural, and though Ryushi was no judge of art, he could see that it was a very accomplished piece. It covered one wall, thousands of tiny, flat stones in different colours picking out the shapes depicted within. His disbelieving eyes ranged over it from end to end, scanning every detail, each new sight bringing with it a fresh stab of horror.

It was the sacking of Osaka Stud.

Ryushi felt sick. There were the King's war-wyverns, sweeping through the air as the Artillerists on their backs unleashed deadly force-bolts into the ruined buidings below. There was the twisted, smoking wreck of the stables, where Ty had so nearly died and where dozens of their father's wyverns had been massacred. There were Kia, Elani and himself, fleeing in the distance on the back of the bull wyvern. And there was Takami, the central pivot around which the rest of the picture swirled, his nodachi sword held high above his head, about to strike down Banto, who was kneeling in the picture as he never had in real life.

Takami was *proud* of it.

Ryushi felt anger suffuse every pore of his body.

He was trembling with fury, his skin reddening under the rush of hatred that followed in its wake. Takami was *gloating* about what he'd done. He had actually commissioned a mural to commemorate the moment when he sold his honour for riches and power, the day when he'd rounded up his whole family and had them executed. Certain details had been changed: he was no longer hiding behind a silver mask, for one thing, as he had been when Ryushi witnessed him slaying their father. But the rest of the scene, apart from his father's kneeling, had been faithfully represented.

He was *proud* of it, Ryushi repeated to himself in horrified amazement. Actually *proud* of it. What kind of creature was he, that their kind father Banto had raised, that they had once called brother? What kind of soulless viper? What kind of *evil*?

He turned away, squeezing his eyes shut hard.

"Pretty messed up, huh?" Whist said tactfully. Blink *whuffed* softly in agreement.

"Show me where he sleeps," Ryushi said through gritted teeth.

"You look riled, kid," Whist said with a grin. "Come on, then. Not far now."

They went on through the corridors for a short while. Ryushi was becoming emboldened about his chances now, for they had been passed several times by a Kirin servant or retainer and once by a Dominion maid, and he had not been recognized yet. His hair was longer, he supposed, and he wore different clothes now. There would be no accurate pictures of him, only a vague description. Seventeen winters, a lean Dominion boy with blond hair . . . it might be applied to dozens of people within the keep. The only danger lay in crossing paths with someone who knew him, but Takami had seen to it that most of them had gone back to the earth. Occasionally, people glanced at the weapons that he and Whist carried openly; but it was mere curiosity, for all nobles and their retainers were allowed to possess weapons in a thane's house. They knew well what Aurin and the Jachyra would do if they were ever foolish enough to use them.

The mural. It kept flashing into Ryushi's head, appearing in every corner of his mind, filling his thoughts. He tried to bottle his rage, for his fierce expression was hardly helping them stay anonymous, but he did not have Kia's gift for suppressing her anger. Instead, his hands gripped into fists, he followed Whist until he was brought to a stop outside a small, carven door in an alcove, nondescript and positioned to be out of the way.

"This isn't it, surely," Ryushi said, looking over the wychwood frame.

"What, the thane's bedroom? *Please*. This is just the vapour-room."

"Why are we—" Ryushi began, but Whist cut him off with a hiss.

"You think Takami's bedroom isn't going to be *guarded*? Are you *dumb*?" He sighed, and Blink looked at him quizzically. "Sometimes I think I'm the only one making any effort."

"Then why don't *you* kill him?" Ryushi said sarcastically.

"Somehow, I don't think you'd let me even if I tried," Whist replied blandly. "And besides, what reward would I get then? I don't care whether Takami lives or dies, as long as I get my deal."

"If Takami lives, then I won't be around to have a deal *with*," Ryushi said irritably.

"I know," Whist replied. "Why else d'you think I'm doing all your work for you? Now shut up and get inside."

"You go first," Ryushi said.

Whist hesitated a moment. "Still don't trust me, huh? Okay, fine." He pushed open the door to the vapour-room and stalked in, his dog slinking behind him. Ryushi followed warily.

The room was small and bare, its only features being a large, cast-iron brazier in the centre of the room and a multitude of ornamentally-wrought grilles around the upper edge of the walls. The brazier was full of fresh coals, cold and unused.

Ryushi shut the door behind them with a soft click, keeping his eyes on Whist.

"These grilles go to all the master bedrooms," Whist said, motioning with his gloved hand. "They put water mixed with all kinds o' herbs on the coals, and it filters through to the rooms."

"What kind of herbs?"

"Sometimes just things to make the room smell

nice," Whist said, shrugging. "Sometimes aphrodisiacs, if they're in that kinda mood. Sometimes narcotics. You can shut off different grilles so only some of the rooms get the benefit. 'S very clever, really."

"What about poison gas? Couldn't you just take out the whole of the Maar nobles with the right ingredient thrown on the coals?"

"You got a sick mind, you know that?" Whist commented, cocking an eyebrow at him. "Anyway, they thought of it. See that door? Machinist lock on it. When the brazier's on to heat the coals, the door stays shut. Some kinda sensor. It's supposed to be a measure to make sure someone watches the brazier at all times when it's on, so no one gets too much of whatever they're using; but it also means that the guys who get paid to do this have to sit around and breathe whatever they're pumping through the system. I mean, they get masks and stuff, but nothing a hundred per cent, y'know? You should see the state of some of those guys after a heavy narc session." He shook his head in mock-disgust. "Anyway, point is, you try and gas someone, you gas *yourself* too. Or you're locked in long enough for the bodies to be discovered and you to get caught and executed. They don't miss much here."

Ryushi looked up at the grilles, bored with the explanation now. "And one of these leads to Takami's bedchamber," Ryushi stated. His tone was sceptical enough to get a response out of Whist.

"Hey, don't go thinkin' it was *easy* clearing a route from here to your bro – to Takami's bedchamber," he protested. Blink raised his ears. "Those ventilation ducts are so loaded with traps, you wouldn't get halfway before you got caught out by *something*. Took me two cycles to disarm every little trick between here and there; I'd like a bit of appreciation, huh?"

"You'll get your appreciation when Takami's dead and we're outta here," Ryushi said. "Now which one is it? And you know that you'll be going first, don't you?"

"Figures," Whist grumbled. He clambered up and pulled loose a grate. It came away easily in his hands, evidence that it had been previously worked on, unlike the others that were set deep in stone.

"You put a lot of preparation into this," Ryushi observed.

"Like I said," he grunted, hauling himself into the shaft. "When I have a plan, it *works*. What I didn't mention was all the cursed legwork that goes into making it turn out that way. Blink, you stay here and follow when we get through."

Blink hunkered down, his head on his forepaws, and scratched his haunch absently with a hind leg.

The vent was narrow and restrictive, barely wider than their shoulders. It was too tight to kneel, so they lay on their bellies with their arms forward and crawled on their elbows, thighs and hips. The interior was mercifully made of smooth metal, so it did not chafe as badly as it might have; but even so, Ryushi found their going slow and uncomfortable. He cast his mind back to the days when he and Kia used to explore the mountain caves back home, often squeezing through tunnels that were barely wider than these ducts. It calmed him slightly.

At first, he could see little but the soles of Whist's boots, his trousers and the three silver ovals of his spirit-stones in his painted back. But as they progressed, he began to see evidence of the traps Whist had spoken of. Here, a curved spring-blade in the floor of the duct had to be gently pushed down so they could wriggle past it; had it not already been sprung, it would have slashed across the belly or throat of an intruder. A little further on, a dry click made him jump, and something jerked near Whist's shoulder. "Poison darts," he said unconcernedly. "Course, a poison dart mechanism with all the darts removed don't make much of a threat."

By the time they reached the grille at the end of the duct, Ryushi wholeheartedly believed what Whist had said. He would not have got even halfway to Takami's bedroom before something killed him.

In the bedchamber beyond the grille, it was pitch dark. Even the windows were covered, with only the faintest line of the grey light from outside showing where they were. They could see nothing.

Whist pushed the grille out of its setting and passed it back to Ryushi. "Bring that with you when you come through; we'll need to replace it, so he doesn't think anything's amiss when he comes in." With that, he wormed his glowstone out of his pocket and unwrapped it. The pale orange glow drove back the darkness a little, sending long, wavering shadows lunging out of the furniture in the room. Whist clambered around and made the short drop down into the room; Ryushi followed him, his eyes alert.

From what he could see, the room was opulent without being garish. Small, low tables stood about, with bowls full of delicate white ornamental pebbles on them, their colour turned apricot by the light of the glowstone. He could almost make out the edge of a fine bed, somewhere in the centre. Wardrobes stood all around, but thankfully no mirrors that he could see.

Whist was quietly replacing the grille, when Ryushi suddenly whirled at a movement from the edge of the light, his sword ringing free of his scabbard.

"Just Blink," Whist said, without turning around. "You'd better hope the guards outside didn't hear that."

The dog padded over to his master. Ryushi looked around the room. It was so dark, he couldn't even locate where the main door was. For a time, he stayed tense, his sword held ready before him; then, when there was no indication that the noise had been heard, he relaxed a little.

"Thick doors," Whist said, talking at normal conversational volume. "They can't hear anything. Don't worry about it."

Ryushi suddenly shifted the edge of his sword, swinging it round so it hovered a centimetre from Whist's throat. Blink growled, his hackles raising and his shoulders bunching. Whist looked at him calmly.

"I will never trust you," Ryushi said. "If I kill Takami, then I'll fulfil our deal. But I'll never trust you. And if this is an ambush –"

"Oh, get real," Whist said impatiently, pushing his sword aside with his armoured glove. "Enough with the posturing. You've got enough spirit-stones in your spine to blow half this keep to pieces. Put your sword away. I'm not stupid enough to try and betray you here."

Ryushi hesitated, then sheathed his blade again. He was sweating with the tension. Making a bargain with a person such as this had left his nerves frayed.

Whist squatted down next to Blink and stroked his back roughly, calming him down. The dog reluctantly quieted, the threatening rumble in his chest gradually dying. And then Whist looked up again, a mocking smile on his lips.

"Unless, of course," he added, "the reward was suitably worthwhile."

"*No!*" Ryushi cried, sensing what was coming and lunging at him, but the room was suddenly plunged into darkness as Blink disappeared along with Whist and the glowstone he held.

"*Whist! I'll kill you!*" he shouted in anger at the emptiness, stumbling backwards and banging the backs of his knees against a low table with a crash. He was blind, and without a glowstone. Panic welled within him.

Betrayed. Get out. Escape.

He could not possibly suppose that Takami did

not know of his presence now. He was trapped here, in the dark. And now, from the endless black all around him, he could hear the sound of a door creaking gently open; a thin door, like that of a wardrobe. And a soft footfall, from another side of the room.

He couldn't fight them here. It was time to make his own exit.

Gritting his teeth, he called upon the power of the Flow, stored in his spirit-stones, willing it forth into his hands to unleash upon something, anything, to make an escape route for himself. Maybe he could hold enough back this time so that he would not drain himself totally. He'd done it before, he could –

But nothing was happening. His stones were not responding. Like a dry-retch, the sensation and feeling were right, but there was nothing coming out. He could feel the energy, still stocked up in the batteries along his spine; but he could not *release* it.

The stones! he thought in panic. *The ornamental pebbles! They're* Damper *stones, like they used on Kia in Os Dakar.*

24

That was when he realized the full extent of the trap he had been let into. Robbed of power and blind, he could not hope to beat whoever or whatever prowled around in the sea of inky darkness. Perhaps they were Kirins, for Kirin eyes could make the most of a tiny scrap of available light in much the same way as cats could. Perhaps they were Jachyra, for who knew what they could do?

He held his sword out before him and prayed it was the former, his ears straining for a sound, any sound.

The only thing he heard was the *whoosh* of a blowpipe before feeling the sting on his cheek as the dart bit; and after that there was nothing.

2

Our Memory is Eternal

Outside the settlement of the Koth Taraan, the Parakkans sat around the flickering phoenix of a newly emerging fire, watching it lapping tentatively between the damp nest of sticks that were piled up around it. Ty had been trying for some time to get the mist-soaked wood to catch, but to no avail. In the end, Gerdi had offered him a small dose of clear liquid that he carried in a little flask, hidden in one of his many pockets. It had flamed up eagerly, and the combination of that and some tinder that Kia had miraculously managed to keep dry in her pack got the fire going at last.

"What *is* that stuff, anyway?" Hochi asked, from where he had been watching near by. Gerdi started, not realizing he had been there.

"Err . . . it's medicinal, that's all," he replied with a nervous grin.

"Medicinal?" Hochi cried. "I know what *that* means. Give me that flask; you're too young."

"No way, fat guy," Gerdi said, leaping to his feet. "You'll just drink it all yourself!"

"I said give it to me!" Hochi shouted, chasing after the young Noman boy as he disappeared from the mud banks of the marsh and into the trees. Kia and Ty listened to Hochi crash after him for a while, until the sounds faded.

"I'm not sure I think much of their hospitality," Kia said after a moment, glancing back at the Koth Taraan's settlement, out in the murky lake. They were still clad in the wet clothes that they had set out in, and covered in smears of mud. It was useless trying to wash it off in the brackish swamp-water of the lake; that only gave them clean skin for new spatters and patches to appear on.

"They're suspicious, that's all," Ty said. "It's not like they've had much contact with strangers, is it?"

"Even so, though," Kia said, poking idly at the

fledgling fire with a spare stick, "it's kinda rude that they won't even let us stay inside, where it's warm."

After their audience with the Koth Macquai, they had been returned to the tender care of their escorts, who had told them in no uncertain terms that they would have to remain outside the settlement until someone came to fetch them. The Koth Macquai had promised to think on what they had said; but how long it would be before they got a reply, they had no idea.

"You're judging them by our standards, Kia," Ty said. "They probably don't even know what *rude* is. They're just wary; they don't want us near them until they decide whether they trust us or not." He paused. "And besides, they don't know whether we're really dangerous. Would *you* let a bunch of Keriags stay in Base Usido, no matter how well guarded they were?"

She smiled. "I guess not." Then she added: "But I wouldn't make them sit on a mud-bank for hours, either."

"No, you'd just put them in a cage with

manacles attached to every available joint," Ty replied.

She shuffled round the edge of the fire and nestled up to Ty, and together they sat watching the fire.

"You think they'll help us out?" he said.

She sighed. "I don't know, Ty. I can't see that we've given them much reason to. We've got no leverage, nothing to offer them really. I just wanted to be doing *something*, y'know? Something that might make a bit of a difference, something that'll . . . I dunno, give Parakka a *chance*." She frowned. "You think I'm just clinging to a false hope or something?"

"Stop picking yourself to pieces," he told her. "It's the best idea anyone's had so far to deal with Aurin. And look, you were *right* about the Koth Taraan. I mean, this is a whole undiscovered culture we've found. That's gotta be worth something."

"Maybe they were undiscovered for a reason," Kia said. "Maybe they wanted to keep it that way."

"Yeah, well," Ty replied. "Things are tough all

over. And you and me both know that nobody can hide for ever."

Kia made a faint noise of agreement.

Jaan wandered the marshes, careful not to stray too far from the settlement in case he got lost. He was used to his own company. He had been born with an unfortunate set of features that showed his halfbreed blood clearly, and he had been largely shunned because of it. He had got over the unfairness of it all long ago; some halfbreeds looked so close to purebreeds that they could live perfectly normal lives if their parentage was not known, and it was just his bad luck that he was such an equal mix of Kirin and Dominion stock that he was clearly neither. Yellow irises, coffee-coloured skin, broad, blocky features; there was no way he could hide it from the world. He had simply had to learn to numb himself.

He hadn't known his father, but he suspected that he had been of the desert-folk in the south of the Dominions. Their mother had found brief solace in the arms of a man like that after Peliqua's father had died of whiplash fever – a

Kirin ailment characterized by bright white welts that appeared across the back and chest of the sufferer. She had never spoken of him, but Peliqua had been old enough to remember vague details. The Dominion man disappeared soon after, taking his secrets with him. Perhaps he had been a Resonant; how else could he have turned up in Kirin Taq? It didn't matter. It did mean, of course, that Peliqua and Jaan were technically only half-siblings, but Peliqua refused to call him anything but a brother. To her, his parentage didn't matter.

Unfortunately, the world was sadly lacking in people to share that opinion. As if the prejudice between Kirin and Dominion folk was not bad enough, Jaan had been forced to contend with it from both sides. It was this, he suspected, that led him to join Parakka when the chance arose. It was an organization composed of both Kirin and Dominion-folk, and professed to allow no discrimination between them. In general, this was true, although there were still odd individuals who had difficulty shedding their old mistrusts and hatreds that had been hammered into them since birth. But Jaan thought it ironic, really; the catalyst for Kirins and Dominion-folk working in harmony was that Parakka were so desperately outnumbered that they couldn't *afford* to discriminate.

What a state of affairs, he thought to himself, brushing aside a vine and plodding through the mushy, damp grass between the trees. And now there's the Koth Taraan, who've done their best to stay out of it. Sensible decision. Why involve yourself in something so *stupid*?

((Your minds are alien to us)) came a voice in his head, accompanied by an indigo shower of puzzlement. *((We cannot see them as we can our own))*

Jaan looked around, and there was one of them, standing less than a metre away from him. For such huge creatures, they moved stealthily and hid themselves well in the wetland terrain.

"I thought you'd turn up," he said. It was the same one that had talked to him before. He didn't know how he knew; maybe it was something in the shade of the colours that crossed his mind when it spoke.

((How did you know?))

"Just a feeling."

The creature turned its head to one side a little, studying him with its wide eyes of endless black. It was fully twice his height, dwarfing Jaan in its presence; yet Jaan felt strangely unafraid as he stood before it, the wetland mists curling around their feet.

He brushed back an errant rope of thick hair from his face and met its gaze. "What did you mean before, when you said you can see your own minds?"

((Each individual shares the thoughts of the Brethren. We are open to each other))

"Like the Keriags?"

A dark rill of displeasure skated over the surface of his mind. ***((We are not like the Keriags. The Keriags have no minds of their own. Their queen is the hive-mind, and the drones are merely her eyes and claws))***

"Sorry," Jaan said, sensing he had insulted the other. A light blue, cleansing wave of forgiveness was his reward. He took a step back and sat down at the twisted base of an old and warped tree, resting on the wet grass. The Koth Taraan settled its huge frame, reverting to its neutral stance.

"Why did you talk to me, out of everyone?" he asked at length.

((Your situation is not dissimilar to our own)) came the reply.

Jaan hesitated. "I . . . don't understand."

((You are neither Kirin nor Dominion stock. You are not accepted by either. Yet you live alongside both. And you maintain your own personal, private culture, without feeling the need to be one or the other)) There was a pause, broken by the howling of some marsh-beast in the murky distance and the incessant drip of water. **((The Koth Taraan have kept themselves segregated for hundreds of years. We are afraid of losing what we have. Our identity. The culture of our people))**

Jaan was faintly disturbed by the creature's stark bluntness, but he listened as it went on.

((The Koth Macquai and the elder Brethren believe that this is the way it should stay. They fear that contact with the Kirin folk will result in our culture being crushed under them))

"They're probably right," Jaan said. "At least at the moment." He found it strange that he should feel so at ease in a conversation with a creature so utterly alien to him, especially as communication had never been his strong point. But he was fascinated by the colours that doused the Koth Taraan's speech, and the directness of its words, both figuratively and literally; after all, they were certainly not passing through the medium of his ears on the way to his brain.

((The younger Brethren among us believe that this is what will happen if we do not make contact. Your Kia-Brethren's words were what we had feared for some time. This King Macaan will eventually find us, or his child, or her children after her. If we are unprepared, we will be beaten, and our histories lost for ever)) It turned its glittering eyes up to the thick, dark foliage above them. *((Taacqan was a great teacher to us. The elder ones distrusted him, but we who are younger listened to what he had to say. He told us how Macaan had destroyed and suppressed the histories of the Dominions and Kirin Taq. He fears the knowledge that history*

brings with it. He rules through ignorance)) The creature looked back at Jaan. *((You have seen our recording-walls. But we do not need them. Our memory is eternal. Macaan could not make us ignorant by destroying them. For Macaan to erase our history, he would have to destroy the Koth Macquai. We cannot allow that))*

Our memory is eternal? The Koth Macquai had mentioned that earlier. Jaan was about to ask about it, when the implication of the creature's last words made him sit up straighter. "Are you saying you'll help us?"

((We cannot. Not without the Koth Macquai's permission))

"But does he know about all that you've said?"

A rainbow of silent laughter. *((Of course. Just as each of us knows about the conversation we are now having. We are not Keriags. We are individuals. Each of us has their own thoughts and opinions. But we cannot keep them secret from our Brethren, in the way you humans can))*

"Yeah, well *that's* a talent that's not all it's cracked up to be," Jaan muttered, vaguely bitter.

Secrets and withheld information were half the reason they were in this situation in the first place. Then, at that moment, a thought occurred to him.

"The Koth Taraan and the Keriags used to be the same breed, didn't they?" he said. He knew that the Koth Taraan did not like to be reminded of the fact, but it was suddenly necessary to reiterate it.

((You have been told as much)) A soft swipe of unhappy blue, annoyed black and puzzled purple rode on the back of its words.

"Then can you *talk* to them?"

((We have no wish to)) came the carefully considered reply.

"Does that mean you *can*?" Jaan asked, excited.

((Perhaps)) it said after a time. *((It has been lifetimes since we have tried))*

"Then couldn't you –?" he began, but for the first time the Koth Taraan interrupted him, barging in on his speech with its thoughts, sheathed in the iron grey of firm insistence.

((We will not. Do not pursue that line of thinking, human child. It will lead you nowhere))

Jaan fell quiet, but he was not chastened. That particular piece of information was a victory beyond anything he had expected to come from this conversation. Securing their cooperation was a step that could be handled later. But if the Koth Taraan could *talk* to the Keriags . . . what if the Keriags *themselves* could tell them what Aurin's power was over them? What if –?

The creature suddenly raised itself again, its massive plates of armour seeming to expand as it did so. *((The decision has been made))* it said suddenly. *((The Koth Macquai has reached a decision. Return to the others. You will be informed))*

Jaan got to his feet, rubbing uselessly at the wet patches on his legs. "Can't you tell me?"

((No)) came the simple reply. Then it almost seemed to soften, and leaned a little closer to the half-breed boy. *((What is your name, human child?))*

"Jaan," he said. "What's yours?"

((The Koth Taraan do not have names))

"But we humans need them," he said with a faint smile. "It's a side-effect of this individual isolation thing you were talking about. I need to call you something."

*((**What would you have me be called among humans?**))* A faint sparkle of intrigue and amusement.

"Iriqi," Jaan said, without hesitation.

*((**Iriqi**))* it repeated. *((**Then that is what you may call me**))* With that, it turned and lumbered away into the wetlands, heading back towards the settlement. Jaan watched it go with his yellow eyes, still unable to fathom the mind of the creature that had seemed to take such an interest in him. After a short time, he suddenly remembered what Iriqi had said, and started quickly back for the camp.

The decision had been made. What was it to be?

"You named it after our *dog*?" Peliqua cried in disbelief. Gerdi was howling with laughter next to her, thumping the muddy ground with his fist and holding his ribs with his other hand.

"What was I supposed to do?" Jaan protested. "I've got a ten-foot high creature standing in front of me asking me to give it a name. I didn't exactly have time to come up with something appropriate. I just said the first thing that popped into my head."

"But your *dog*?" Gerdi screamed through his tears, still having seizures in the mud. Hochi regarded him much as he would regard a smear of half-eaten bread on the the floor of his hut.

"No, perhaps he was right to call it that," Peliqua said thoughtfully, reverting to her usual habit of swinging everything to a positive angle. "It's a fitting tribute. We loved our old dog, before its time came."

"Yeah, I'm sure the Koth Taraan will be *so* impressed when they find out," Gerdi put in, but his words were mangled by his hysterical laughter and nobody could make much sense of them.

"Can we drop it, okay? It's done now. I shouldn't have bothered telling you," Jaan said sullenly, pulling his hood up over the thick nest of his hair and lapsing back into silence.

"Okay guys, enough," Kia said, from the other side of the campfire. "Here they come." She motioned towards the small procession of Koth

Taraan that were approaching across the flat bridge between the settlement and the mud bank on the edge of the lake. She was not much in the mood for laughing. Gerdi didn't seem to appreciate how important the Koth Macquai's decision was. Even though the information Jaan had gleaned from Iriqi had put a fresh sheen of hope on things, it would still all be for nothing if the Koth Macquai refused to help them. A simple yes or no answer, but it could be the catalyst that saved or doomed Parakka.

She found herself barely able to breathe as she stood up. Ty took her hand and squeezed it reassuringly. Even that did little good. They all waited, still caked in mud and looking more like vagabonds than diplomats, as the three Koth Taraan came to a halt at the end of the bridge, in front of them. Gerdi was still biting his lip and chuckling, but he had positioned himself well out of Hochi's way, so there was nothing the big man could do to shut him up.

((The Koth Macquai has reached a decision)) they were informed. The short pause was strung taut with anticipation. *((It has been deemed that*

this issue is too delicate to commit ourselves to, even tentatively, without knowing more about yourselves. Therefore, one of you is invited to submit yourself to a test to prove your worth to us))

"I'll do it," said Kia, without even waiting to hear what it was. The creatures turned their eyes upon her.

((Then come with us now. Alone. The test begins at once))

3

Strike and Counterstrike

A long tunnel. There's an archway ahead, leading into a huge room, filled with the hushed whispers of a hundred people. Steady strides carry him past the finely-crafted panelling on the walls, beneath the green, fluted tiling of the ceiling. His footsteps are accompanied by the tramp of two Guardsmen, walking by each elbow, propelling him onward, inexorably, towards the archway.

And then Ryushi walked out into the Great Hall of his brother Takami's keep.

It was like a small amphitheatre in design. A large, central floor area of white and blue tiles had a raised dais and an ornate seat like a throne at its head. Around its oval perimeter, a smooth wall of white rose to a height of perhaps twenty feet; and above that were three tiers of seats, carved from fine wood and plush with cushions, upon which sat the members of Takami's court. Ryushi looked around them fearlessly as he entered, meeting their gazes. They were almost exclusively Kirin, and they watched him with a mixture of curiosity, sympathy and disdain in their white eyes.

The Guardsmen had stopped at the archway and taken up position there, so he was left to walk out into the hall alone, his boots tapping hollow as he came. He had no weapons, but nor was he chained. A Damper Collar was affixed around his neck, the single stone of frosty white set into the thin, strong metal at his throat. Ryushi made his way a short distance across the echoing room, his head held high, determined not to give the onlookers the satisfaction of seeing him shamed; and there he stopped, waiting expectantly.

Two swords stood point down in the centre of the room, supported by a metal bracket; his own, and the longer blade of the nodachi used by his brother. Beyond them, sitting on the chair that was so nearly a throne, was Takami, clad in his elegant green armour, a cruel smile twisting his face. He was framed against a hanging tapestry, draped across the wall behind him, bearing a stylized depiction of a wyvern. Had Ryushi been in a mind to notice, he might have thought that it seemed curiously out of place here, incongruous amid the rest of the fine décor. It didn't hang quite right, either; almost as if it had been put up in some haste. But he was focused only on his brother, and in the silence that filled the room, he glared at Takami with naked hate in his eyes.

"Ryushi, Ryushi," Takami sighed. "When will you ever learn?" He got to his feet, and his next appeal was addressed half to Ryushi and half to the surrounding court, playing up to his audience. "Don't you remember last time we met, you tried to give me a lecture on *real life*, brother? It seems you know less than you think you do; for here we are again, and this time you've brought yourself right into my hands."

"I also seem to remember that last time we met, I beat you soundly," Ryushi said. If Takami wanted this to be in public, he'd *make* it public. "And I would have killed you then, had not one of

Macaan's little helpers been there to drag you out of trouble."

Ryushi had expected Takami to show at least a flicker of anger at the reminder of his humiliation, but he shrugged it off with an insouciant smile. "Ah, but you're bringing up the past; and what really matters is the here and now. You see, *I'm* a thane here. I have money, I have power, I want for nothing. While *you* are still grubbing around in the dirt, putting your life in peril for the sake of a misplaced sense of honour. Are you still sure you made the right choice? Has this last year been as easy for you as it has for me? I doubt it, little brother. Really I do."

"Well, no, it's not been easy," Ryushi said, his voice loud enough to carry around the room. "But then, perhaps, I've been doing something more constructive than getting fat from Aurin's teats and commissioning murals to celebrate murdering my defenceless family."

A shocked outcry arose from the upper galleries; not at the second slight, but at the first. To insult the Princess was a death sentence. Ryushi didn't care. Treason was a way of life to him now; he'd incurred the death sentence many times over.

"I see that mixing with the dirt and beetles has coarsened your vocabulary," Takami said, strolling down the steps of the dais. "That's one more reason to end your pitiful life."

"You need reasons now?" Ryushi asked. "You didn't need a reason to execute women and children back at Osaka Stud, did you? Or to kill your own father because you dared not face him in a fair fight."

"*Please*, little brother," Takami said. "Look at where you are. You're hardly in a position to make effective taunts. But as to a *fair fight*. . ." He strolled over to where the two swords stood in the bracket. "Well, that is exactly what I'm offering you. You see, I do owe you for beating me back in the Ley Warren, and as you've so graciously allowed yourself to be tricked into coming to my keep, it is now time to even the score."

"Take this Damper Collar off me and we'll see a fair fight," Ryushi said.

"Unlikely," Takami said. "However, I will make

you this concession." He motioned at another archway, and a page crossed the room towards him. He knelt down on one knee, keeping his eyes fixed on his brother, and allowed a Damper Collar to be fixed to his own neck. For a wild moment, Ryushi pictured seizing his blade and striking him down right then; without his powers, he was weaponless. But it was madness. Takami undoubtedly had several Guardsmen with their halberds trained on him, ready to unleash their deadly force-bolts. And besides, such a victory would have no honour, and would sully his father's memory. He could beat Takami again, he told himself. Fairly.

But somehow, he doubted it would really be that easy.

When Takami was sure the Collar was secure, he stood back up again. Slowly, he drew his nodachi from the free-standing bracket, savouring the sound of metal sliding over metal as it came. The crowd above, minor nobles and other dignitaries or people seeking to curry favour within the thane's court, were utterly silent. Only the faint muttering of the torches that lit the room brightly could be heard as Takami stepped back and Ryushi reached forward to take his own blade. The page scooped up the bracket and scampered off, back into the shadow of the archway; and then there was only Takami and Ryushi in the arena of the Great Hall, their eyes locked together, each waiting for the other to make the first strike, *daring* them.

"When I kill you," Ryushi said suddenly, "what then?"

Takami laughed tersely. "*If* you kill me," he repeated, smirking, "you'll still be executed. But at least you'll have the satisfaction of watching me die first. Isn't that enough for you?"

"Plenty," Ryushi said; and a moment later he swung his sword up and low, hoping to take Takami's knuckles off his sword-hand. It was an awkward angle to block from, but Takami rose to the challenge, shifting his blade to repel the strike with a harsh clash of steel. The gallery gasped as Takami responded by dropping into a leg sweep, his armour hampering his movement not one bit; but Ryushi jumped over the scything arc of his heel and brought his sword down in a two-handed smash. Takami had been ready, though; he knocked the blade aside as he rose and brought the elbow of his free arm viciously up into Ryushi's jaw. The clack of his teeth jarring together echoed around the arena, and he staggered back a way, allowing Takami time to compose himself.

"As you see," Takami said, "I haven't spent the last year letting my fighting skills get stagnant."

Ryushi spat blood, staining his lips a deep red. "You know, I'm curious," he said. He wanted Takami to talk for a moment, to allow him to shake off the effects of the last blow. "What was really the deal with you and Whist?"

"I imagine it was very much different to what he told you," Takami observed, closing in and circling again. "My Guardsmen found him, half-starved near Os Dakar. After he told me what he knew – and we had a lot of false starts that I had to persuade him out of; you know, he's terrible for lying –"

"Really?" Ryushi said sarcastically.

Takami made a small, tight smile in response. "Anyway, when they told me you were dead, I never believed them. I mean, no body? You just disappeared off the veldt outside the Ley Warren? Very impressive, but hardly conclusive. So I held on to Whist in my dungeons for a while. I knew he'd turn out to be useful one day. Then, when I heard you'd been sighted alive, I knew it was time to bring him out. A simple trade; his freedom, if he would deliver you to me. And if he tried to run, I had Aurin's permission to set the Jachyra on him. That kept him on a leash, well enough." He paused. "Of course, we had to make it all convincing. I made sure everyone knew who he was, and would pretend he was a familiar member of the keep. I allowed you to get into the land-train depot and past the checkpoint. And we set up a false bedroom, disarmed the traps in the ventilation ducts, and led you into it."

"That's a lot of detail. Congratulations," Ryushi said, never taking his eyes off his brother.

"We knew you'd be suspicious from the start, especially as it was Whist we were sending. But who else would you believe could get you into my keep? Certainly not—"

He cried out as Ryushi suddenly flicked the

51

point of his sword-blade up. His heavier nodachi was not fast enough to block it, but he managed to pull his head back quickly enough so that instead of cutting into his throat, it sliced a short, stinging line up his chin. The gallery thundered in anger, but Ryushi only smiled.

"You lose concentration when you boast, Takami. Arrogance is a weakness in combat. By the way, how's your shoulder healing up?"

Takami's eyes filled with anger as he touched his chin with his armoured glove and saw the blood on his fingertips; the reminder of the injury he had sustained last time they met was just salt in the wound.

"You'll pay dearly for that," he promised.

"I'm bored of your threats, Takami," Ryushi said, his tone full of disdain. "Let's get this over with, shall we? Father's spirit is impatient for his vengeance, and frankly, I'm sick of looking at you."

"Very well, little brother," Takami replied, his voice grating. "We will finish this now, once and for all."

Their swords met, parrying high, low, sweeping

in short arcs of death as the wielders danced and weaved between them. The air sang with the punching chimes of their combat, flurries of blows exchanged, strike and counterstrike, feint and dodge. Both of them had been trained since early childhood towards mastery of their weapons; and while neither had the experience to make them truly great fighters, they were still swift and deadly. Both fought with a viciousness that sometimes slipped just beyond its reins, making them occasionally overswing or lunge too hard – for neither had Kia's iron self-control – but the two were evenly matched, and the combat was frighteningly close. Those in the galleries held their breath as the brothers matched swords again and again, but neither could find the crucial advantage that they needed to land the fatal strike on the other.

Eventually they broke apart, panting, their backs heaving as they leaned low over their weapons, facing the other.

"You can't beat me," Ryushi said with a fierce grin, and what was more, he believed it. The anger and adrenalin surging around his body made him feel indestructible, and as he stood with his sweat-soaked fringe dripping into his eyes, he knew without a doubt that he would kill Takami, here and now, and whatever happened after would not matter any more. His honour would be satisfied.

"Oh, but little brother," Takami replied. "I haven't even *begun* to fight yet."

They launched back into each other, leaping together and clashing in mid-air; but this time, as their swords hit, Ryushi felt an unexpected force behind his brother's blow. His sword recoiled hard, bruising his hands and almost making him drop it. He landed and rolled as Takami sent a backhand swipe at his neck. The blade passed harmlessly over his head, and he flipped to his feet again; but he was unable to conceal the sudden worry on his face.

So strong . . . where is it coming from?

But Takami was already attacking again, his nodachi blurring into a slash at his ribs. Ryushi stepped aside easily and glanced it away, but even that small contact made his sword jump in his hands. The metal of the hilt was getting uncomfortably warm, too. He had thought it was the heat from his palms, but now he realized it could not be. His sword was getting hotter.

Another blow from Takami; and this one he barely fended off, even with his whole weight behind the parry. There was a glint in Takami's eyes, an evil triumph on his face; and as the swords parted, just for the briefest of seconds, there was a flicker of green fire that puffed out in the air between them.

Takami was using his spirit-stones. His Damper Collar was a dud. Subtly, underhandedly, so his audience could not see, he was cheating. Ryushi should have known he would never submit to a truly fair fight; where was the sense in risking defeat when he could simply execute his brother and be done with it? No, he was exacting retribution; his reputation had been damaged by his defeat at the Ley Warren, and he had to redress the balance. To his court, he had heroically offered his brother a chance for an honourable death; but really, he had known what he had been doing all along. The chance he offered was very slim indeed.

But it's still a chance. A lucky strike could end this.

Kill him. For Father.

When next Takami's blade came down, Ryushi's parry was a fake. Keeping his wrist loose, he put no strength into the block, but instead twisted out of the way behind it. Takami's nodachi smashed through his guard much further than Takami had intended, but found only empty air on the other side; Ryushi's blade, capitalizing on the recoil, was already swinging back towards his brother. Takami saw the danger, spinning out of the way, as the bright slash of the sword cut through the torchlight. The combination was enacted faster than the eye could follow, and they seemed to part in slow motion, both suddenly stepping back and away from each other.

For a long second, there was nothing.

Then Takami's howl of pain and anger rose up to fill the Great Hall, and his armoured hand pressed against the side of his head as if it could contain the flow of blood there, running out between his fingers, staining the green metal black. On the floor between them, in a steadily growing puddle of its own blood, was Takami's left ear. The gallery was hushed in horror as they watched him stumble backwards, his eyes wide in disbelief at the evidence of his own mutilation.

"Cut the theatrics," Ryushi said. "If you're gonna cheat, finish me now. But don't pretend you can kill me with honour, my erstwhile brother, because honour is something you'll never have again."

That final goad was all it took. Takami roared, his sword erupting into ochre flame, and he threw himself at his brother, one side of his face stained dark with blood. The first strike was wild, but Ryushi was unable to hit back under the sheer force of his brother's fury. His previous elation had died; he knew now that there was no way to win without his spirit-stones. All he had left was the hope that he could make Takami regret ever giving him the chance to fight for his life.

The second blow, accompanied by a searing arc of fire, swooped past Ryushi's head with a savagery that took him off-guard. He tried to get a counterstrike in, but it was hurried and weak, and Takami's defences turned it aside.

"*Die!*" Takami cried, and then his nodachi was coming down in a double-handed swipe, and though Ryushi knew he could parry it in time he saw what was coming. The two blades met in an explosion of flame, and Ryushi's blade snapped in half under the terrible force. He fell back, his arms numb, his fingers falling open under the shock and the hilt falling free. Hitting the ground heavily, he tried to roll, but his angle was bad and he landed awkwardly, unprepared for the next strike. Not that it would matter now, of course, because –

And then something flashed between them, leaping over Ryushi and crashing into his brother, almost too fast to follow. Then another, and another; and suddenly the gallery was in uproar, shouting and stamping as Ryushi dazedly raised his head and looked. . .

"He is *mine*! He is *mine*!" Takami was screaming, and Ryushi's eyes widened as he saw the scene before him. "*I'll kill you all!*"

+++ **That would be unwise, Takami-kos. Most unwise** +++

Takami was pinned under three Jachyra,

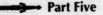

hunched over him like ghouls. The central one he recognized from the assemblage of its metal features; it was the same one that he had faced in the Ley Warren a year ago. It had its finger-claws pressed up against Takami's throat, while its companions controlled his thrashing arms.

+++ **I would kill you before you could summon your power, Takami-kos** +++ Tatterdemalion said through a screen of static. +++ **Princess Aurin is displeased with you, my thane. Very displeased** +++

"Let me go! He took my *ear*! You can't have him!"

+++ **But we can** +++ came the implacable reply. +++ **And you will not prevent us. Your status as a thane of my Princess has already been called into question today. Such an act might well result in you becoming an ex-thane** +++

The way the Jachyra phrased the sentence, along with the stories Ryushi had already heard about those who displeased Aurin, left him in no doubt as to what being an ex-thane meant.

He felt sudden, rough hands on his shoulders and arms, and a moment later he was being dragged up by more of the Jachyra. They surrounded him with their repulsive, musty oil-and-rags smell and their mechanical wheeps and crackles as they held him between them, their disjointed and unnatural bodies arranged around him as a guard, their retractable finger-blades never more than an inch away. If he tried to escape, they would shred him. He remembered what had happened to the defectors on the beach at Mon Tetsaa and swallowed.

Behind Takami's chair of office, the tapestry that had hung there had been torn to pieces, revealing a tall mirror, three times the height of a man and perhaps half that distance in width. Takami had been covering it to hide what he was doing from Aurin's secret police; did that mean that it was not *him* that had planned Ryushi's capture, but Aurin after all?

He had no time to consider the question. Ryushi was dragged roughly towards the mirror, his head swimming in a mixture of elation and terror. He had escaped death once again; but was he heading into something worse?

With his arms held fast, he could not obey his

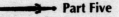

instinct to throw his hands in front of his face as he was pulled towards the hard, cold face of the mirror; but the impact he expected never came, and the last thing he heard before disappearing into his own reflection was Takami's shriek of frustration as he departed.

4

Your Father Nonetheless

Kia stood alone in the slowly churning mist, her skin and clothes soaked from the hot, damp air, fronds of hair plastered to her forehead, cheeks and neck. The hard, uneven floor at her feet was her only point of stable reference in the shifting netherworld that surrounded her, and though the logical side of her mind told itself it knew exactly where she was, it was difficult to convince herself that the emptiness on all sides did not go on for ever.

It was the room of mists, where they had previously met the Koth Macquai. But that time there had been all of them together, and she had had Ty by her side to draw strength from. Now she had no one; the others had been forbidden to enter the settlement with her, and she had been left by her silent escort at the mouth of the ceramic blister that contained the recording-wall that they had admired earlier. She had no idea what she was supposed to be doing, or what the test was that she had agreed to take. Butterflies that felt more like bats thrashed around in her stomach, and she felt cold despite the heat as her nervous mind flitted over the possibilities of the ordeal she might have to face.

But it didn't matter. There had never really been any question about her agreeing. She had to, and she knew it.

Enough. She began to walk forward slowly again. The red, steaming pools of weed-laden water slowly formed at her feet, and she stepped carefully around them. ***((Human child))*** came the voice, suddenly. ***((This way))***

Though the voice had no source that Kia could follow, it was pursued by a strong impression of the location of the Koth Macquai in the room. She blinked in surprise, then automatically turned towards where she had been told to go and plunged onward through the mist.

The Koth Macquai was there, its huge form

describing the outline of a thick, branching tree as it hunkered at the edge of a particularly small pool, only six feet from one irregular side to the other. The antler-like protrusions on its joints and back rattled as it stood taller, acknowledging Kia's arrival. She dropped to one knee and bowed briefly, knowing that the creature did not stand on ceremony but doing it anyway.

((Rise, I ask you)) the Koth Macquai said, faint amusement and indulgence colouring its words. *((Your kind owe no fealty to me))*

Kia didn't comment on that as she got back to her feet, but instead said: "What sort of test would you have me do?"

((You are a brave and reckless one, to take a test without knowing what it entails)) the Koth Macquai stated.

"No," she said. "I just don't have a choice."

((You always have a choice, human child. It is only the limitations you impose on yourself that restrict you))

"Well, those limitations are restricting me pretty good right now," she said, with half a smile. "Tell me about the test. Will I have to fight?"

A sparkling smudge of many colours spread across her mind as the Koth Macquai laughed. *((It is merely a test of character. No physical harm can come to you. We seek only to divine the true motivation behind your proposal, and to know what kind of person it is that brings us such an offer))*

Kia was faintly relieved; after the exhausting journey here and the poor sleep she'd had since, she was in no state for anything physical. "How will you do that? With questions?"

((Questions can be answered falsely)) came the reply, the wide, dark eyes studying her closely. *((The pool. You must immerse yourself in the pool. We will do the rest))*

Kia was hesitant. "The pool?" she asked, looking doubtfully at the murky, steaming water and the gently waving reeds and leaves beneath its surface. The red light that suffused the cavern glowed at its bottom, but the water was too cloudy to see where it came from.

((Do not worry. We have used the pools for many of our generations. They will teach you things. Insights that even you yourself may not

be aware of. Premonitions. Dreams. Hopes and
fears. The pool strips you to nothing, human
child, and leaves only that which cannot be
washed away: the truth))

"The truth," Kia repeated. "I can handle that."

((We shall see. Are you ready, human child?))

Kia took a breath. For a moment, her will
faltered; but she set it rigidly again, allowing
herself no pity. She must do this, she told herself.

"Ready," she said firmly.

The Koth Macquai settled again, compacting
its huge weight down on its haunches so its
massive claws hung over the lip of the pool and
dipped into the water. The chipped sabres that
were its digits were heavily adorned with the
curious rings that Kia had seen the artisans of
the race wearing, except they carried not tools
but simple symbols and pictograms. She
watched, fascinated, as a small, sharp white
glow began to suffuse the deeper red of the
room. In the midst of the Koth Macquai's thin,
unprotected chest, an oval of flesh was burning
bright, a light from something within its body. It
was mesmerizing, the resonance of a million

frozen moments, its radiance carrying with it much more than mere light, but also sound . . . and *memory*.

((Climb into the pool)) the Koth Macquai ordered.

Kia lowered herself until she was sitting on the edge of the pool, with her legs dangling in the water. It was warm as it soaked through her clothes and boots. Well, no matter, they were already wet. With that as her final thought, she slipped into the water, and as her head plunged beneath the surface she felt a sudden, breathless lift in her chest and she was gone.

It was sunny again. The best time of the day, when the morning sun had just crested the eastern mountains and was blasting heat down into the valley. The kitchen had three tall windows that caught the light full on, and on summer days like this one it transformed the room into a haven of cosy, sluggish heat as they breakfasted. They were sitting on benches at a table of smoothed wood, with melting honeycomb and cream in pitchers next to pancakes and scones and glasses of berry water. The floor and walls were of plain, varnished planks, but rugs and pictures kept the room lively, and a stove sat comfortably at one end. Outside, the noises of the workers that had been up with the dawn could be faintly heard, as they busied themselves with the hardest jobs before the ascending heat made them unbearable.

Osaka Stud. It was the best and only place in the world to Kia.

She glanced at Ryushi, who was sitting next to her on the bench. He was eating with characteristic abandon, his face smeared in honey. He stuck his tongue out at her as he caught her gaze, and she punched his thigh underneath the table.

"Don't start, you two," said their mother from where she stood at the stove. Kia gave her twin a poisonous glance and turned away.

Across the table, Calica and Aurin were sitting next to each other, wearing the same immaculate smocks. Both of them had their hair in pigtails, and Kia could tell by the angle of their shoulders that they held hands beneath the tabletop. They were watching her with a combined, unwavering stare, cold and reptilian.

Kia frowned. She had always thought of Aurin as being older than the rest of them, somehow; but here she was, in the flesh, with no more than six winters under her belt. She didn't like playing with either the Princess or her creepy friend. What were they doing here, anyway? This was *her* kitchen, not theirs. She began to get angry. Why were they always muscling in on her? They weren't family. Cuckoos in the nest, that's what they were; and Mother was taken in by them. But Kia knew, alright. She saw through them. They were just there to take what was hers. Well, she wasn't going to let them.

The door to the hallway opened then, and Takami came in. He was as she had always remembered him; towering over them, tall and thin and frighteningly old and mature. He sat down on the bench next to the twin entity of Calica and Aurin, and didn't say anything, just glared disapprovingly at everyone and everything until Kia got bored of watching him.

Instead, she turned her attention to Mother. She

was doing something on the stove, but Kia couldn't see what. That was no surprise; everything her mother did was done in secret. Kia spooned another mound of cream and honey into her mouth, her huge green eyes fixed on their mother's back, and suddenly she felt a terrible desire to see the face of the person at the stove, the *real* face. But when she tried to speak and get her attention, she found that she couldn't, and in the end she gave up trying.

"Father's home," Mother said, without looking up from the stove or turning around.

All of them turned to the door expectantly; but as it swung open, Kia felt an awful wrench somewhere inside her, and time seemed suddenly to decelerate hard. The sun slipped behind a thick cloud and the room darkened. Walking in, as if through syrup, was a lean, dark shadow. Dreamlike, it left streamers of itself behind as it moved, wisps and after-images; and it radiated a chill that had nothing to do with temperature.

She watched in horror as it darted across the room, touching her mother on the shoulder with one crooked finger, and with a sigh she slumped to the ground, dead. Aurin and Calica's eyes followed it dispassionately as it lunged past them to touch Takami in a similar way, and Kia squealed as he seemed to shrivel and gnarl in front of her, becoming twisted and rotten, his eyes bright and cruel like an owl's.

"You're not my father!" she shrieked at the shadow.

"*Not your first father, no,*" it replied in a rasping voice. "*But your father nonetheless.*"

And with that, it reached across the table and grabbed Ryushi by the wrist, picking up his small body effortlessly and carrying him out of the door. Ryushi did not scream or struggle, showing no sign of resistance as he was dragged away from her; but she cried out at the sudden loss, scrambling to her feet and chasing out of the door and into the twilight. For Osaka Stud was gone now, and they ran under the cold eye of the Kirin Taq sun.

She spied the shadow, impossibly fast, streaking away from her with her brother lying calmly in the crook of its arm. She felt a stab of pain, as if someone had thrust a knife in her back and held it there, twisting gradually more and more as the distance between them increased. Desperate to end or at least reduce the agony, she ran after, her tiny feet carrying her across the stony ground, but she could not catch up with him. And then, suddenly, the ground betrayed her, and what had been flat earth suddenly terminated in a clifftop. She wheeled her arms, balancing herself as she skidded to a halt, and then a voice behind her made. . .

. . .her spin and there was Takami, not bent and foul as he had been before but tall and strong, his silver mask on his face, fashioned in the effigy of a spirit howling in despair and agony. She was no longer a child, but back to her natural age, with her bo staff gripped tightly in her hands and her red hair whipping about her face in the salty sea wind. They stood on a pinnacle, a straight finger of rock that thrust out of the raging ocean beneath them. Lowering clouds lashed them with rain, and a howling gale cut around them. Takami was in his green armour, the armour he had worn when he had murdered their father, and he held his nodachi out before him, the long edge crawling with tiny rivulets of water.

With a cry, they struck together, her staff meeting his blade hard. His metal visage was impassive as he sliced at her, making him faceless and anonymous, like Macaan's Guardsmen. She fought him away, her feet steady on the tiny platform of stone that they battled on. There was no urgency in the combat, no excitement or fear; it was as if they were enacting a puppet-play. Each stroke was planned; each stab, each parry, the blade and the staff meeting time and time again as if they were predestined to do so. And the outcome was equally as inevitable. Kia felt hardly even in control of herself as she knocked aside a clumsy strike and hammered the end of her weapon brutally into Takami's armoured shin. His foot slipped back on the wet rock, his sword went wild; and Kia planted her boot in his stomach and shoved.

With a shriek, he stumbled backwards and lost his footing, and at that moment Kia felt control of her body return to her. His mask fell free somehow, his nodachi falling after it into the thrashing sea below; and for the longest of seconds Takami hung on the edge of falling, his arms wheeling, his eyes fixed on hers in an expression of supplication. He was missing an ear.

"Sister! *Please!*" he cried, unable to regain his balance.

Please? Here was the man who had murdered their father, who had killed their family, who had exiled her and Ryushi from the sanctuary of Osaka Stud . . . and he asked her to save his life? When she knew that he was capable of the worst treachery, and that if he lived, he would only continue to hunt them down? When, if their situations were reversed, he would let her fall without a second thought?

Takami pitched backwards, his balance finally lost.

Her arm shot out through the rain and grabbed his, pulling him back from the brink, clasping hard on his gloved. . .

. . .hand in hand with her father, her palm sleepily in his cracked and callused fingers, dozing in the soporific warmth of a blazing fire. It has been a hard day of work and play, and though she hasn't slept in her father's lap for years, she finds herself drowsing now on the big, old armchair that he had brought back from his travels one day. Her mother is talking near by, and though she hears what is being said, it doesn't register in her sleep-fogged mind.

"Look at her, Banto. Fifteen winters old and she still looks like a little girl when she curls up on your lap."

She can feel Banto's smile in his voice. "It does my heart good to see them so happy. Exhausted, but happy. It is my fear that it cannot last much longer. Soon the time will come for Takami to learn about—"

"Banto!" her mother whispers urgently. "She could still hear!"

A pause. "Kia?" her father says, and she can feel the depth of his voice through his broad chest. "Kia?"

She stirs, making a noise of dreamy gibberish. She is asleep, right enough.

"She'll not know a thing," Banto says.

"She could be faking it."

"I'd know."

A sigh from her mother. "I suppose we must leave tomorrow."

For some reason, that sentence evokes a dread in Kia such as she has never felt before. She wants to wake up, wants to scream *No! Don't go!* But she can't.

"I'm sure it'll be okay. It's not as if she's ever been wrong before, is it?"

Her mother shifts uncomfortably in her chair. "This one feels wrong, though."

"You always say that."

"I know. And one time I'll be right." A short laugh. "It's just nerves, I know. These recruitment missions always set me on edge. You never know, you just never. . . I mean, one day Macaan's going to get wise to us, and set us a trap. It could be this one."

"It could," Banto replies. "But we have the best operatives. The best intelligence."

No, don't listen to him, Mother! If you go, you'll never come back to me! If you go, I'll never see you again!

Her mother relaxes. "I suppose so. And like you say, it's not as if Calica's ever been wrong before, is it?"

Calica? Calica!

She opens her eyes and gets up calmly, and as she walks out of the room her parents appear not to notice her. As if sleepwalking, she pushes open the door and heads for the stairs. A single glowstone at the top shines orange light down the steps; she puts one hand on the banister and heads for it. Upstairs is where they are sleeping.

Upstairs is where she will kill Calica.

She sent my mother to die.

At the top there's a bedroom that she's never seen before, much bigger than the rest of them. There are two sleeping-pallets here, each wide enough for two. She can't see well in the darkness, but she knows exactly where she's going. She walks softly over to the bed where Calica's orange-gold hair is visible, framing her sleeping, six-winter face. Without hesitation, she slips her hands around the child's throat and squeezes.

Instantly the world around her becomes a

screeching, scratching mass as Aurin leaps on her, tearing at her, protecting her sibling. She cries out and stumbles back, but Aurin bears her to the floor, and Calica now with her, two frenzied children that thrash and bite and flail and –

Suddenly they stop. Kia opens her eyes. They are watching her again with the cold, reptilian eyes. Aurin is holding out a dagger with a long, curved blade, offering it to her. Numbly, she takes it. Aurin points slowly to the other bed. Kia gets up and walks over to it, and there in the bed is the shadow, the one that stole her brother and killed her mother and replaced her father. The two children watch from the floor as she raises the knife above the sleeping victim.

"Don't, Kia," says a voice at her shoulder, and it's Ty. She turns to look at him, and there he is, gazing earnestly at her, the Pilot's apprentice she once knew, shy and sensitive.

"I have to," she says.

"If you try and kill him, I will die too."

"No," she says, shaking her head. "No, I'll make sure you don't."

And with that, she suddenly plunges the dagger into the face of the shadow in the bed, and the screech it makes as she stabs it again and again seems to go on for ever, ending in a high-pitched. . .

. . .whine of blood in her ears, her lungs aching, and she broke the surface of the pool, gasping for air. The steam and mist around her dulled the sounds of her struggle as she grabbed hold of the edge of the pool and pulled herself out. Fronds of weed lay limply against her neck, falling free as she hauled herself on to the hard, uneven floor of the room in a cascade of water and then lay there, breathing hard, forming a pool of her own.

((Rest, human child)) came the voice of the Koth Macquai, as it slowly raised its claws out of the pool and the white glow in its chest died. *((Taacqan before you suffered much the same fatigue))*

"I . . . failed," Kia panted bitterly.

((In this test, there is no failure. The truth is always a victory))

"Then . . ." she gasped, "what happens . . . now?"

((Now you go back to your lands))

She coughed and raised herself a little, looking into the black eyes of the Koth Macquai as it regarded her impassively. "Your decision. When will we know?"

((The decision has already been made. You have neither the best interests of the Koth Taraan nor of Parakka at heart when you ask us to join you. You seek only to destroy the shadow that dominates your life; the welfare of my Brethren is unimportant to you in comparison. We will not help you))

Kia sagged, slumping back to the floor, the weight of disappointment bearing her down again.

((But do not despair, human child)) it continued, a powdery blue cloud of sympathy engulfing her. *((Your ordeal revealed that you, at least, believe what you say about the threat Macaan poses to us. This corroborates what Taacqan told us some time ago. A proportion of the younger Brethren have made known that*

they would have us send a representative with you, to observe and judge the truth of this for the Koth Taraan))

"Iriqi," Kia said distantly.

((Iriqi)) the Koth Macquai agreed.

5

As Inevitable as Time

Ryushi opened his eyes and wished he hadn't. The hunger was still there, waiting to spring on him the moment his conscious mind was aware enough to recognize it. His stomach had shrunk considerably, but it did little good now. It felt like it was trying to eat itself for want of anything better to digest.

He lay on the hard creamstone floor of his cell, feeling a headache begin to rise at the back of his skull. It was better than lying on the smooth, curved bench that jutted out of the gently rounded wall; since his captors had allowed him no bedding, the only advantage that sleeping there might provide was that he might fall off and break his neck, sparing him whatever was in store for him later.

There was no chance of him getting back to sleep now; his body had already started its insistent clamour for food. He sat up, feeling a wave of lightheadedness clutch at him as he did so, and gave his Damper Collar an experimental tug in case it had somehow loosened in the night. The cell around him was clean and immaculate, a slightly yellowish white. He estimated that he had been here for three cycles by now, but there was no way of telling without a Glimmer shard. It was featureless but for a thin trench against the far wall, flowing with water for his ablutions, and the three tiny oval wind-holes in the elliptical door. These were only big enough for him to fit three fingers through, and looked out on an equally blank and featureless corridor. A single torch burned in a locked and shielded alcove bracket, and was replaced periodically. Occasionally a young Kirin boy brought him a thimble-sized bowl of rice and some water, flanked by two Guardsmen with their deadly halberds trained on him. That was the only sign of life he had seen.

He was a prisoner in Aurin's palace, Fane

Aracq. And he had a nasty suspicion that they were softening him up for something.

Clambering over to the bench, he sat down and rested his face in his hands. He had been so close, *so* close. An inch to the left, and he could have ended it then. Takami would be dead. His honour would be satisfied. So Takami had lost an ear; so what? Ryushi derived a little satisfaction from that, but not enough. Because he'd never get a chance to finish the job now, and so in the end, Takami would get away with it. He felt miserable; and worse, he felt that he had let everyone down. He'd failed to kill Takami, and now he was in Aurin's hands. She had, at last, a genuine Parakkan to play with. One who knew a lot about the operation of the organization. One who would know where they were based.

And she would find out what he knew. He remembered stories Ty had told him, the pain etched on his face, about what Macaan had done to him after he had been captured at Osaka Stud. He did not relish the thought of experiencing that at first-hand. But it was as inevitable as time, and there was nothing he could do to stop it.

Suicide? The thought had crossed and recrossed his mind, each passing leaving deeper footprints. But no, that was no option. It was something his honour would not allow him to do. He had got himself into this situation because even the tiniest chance at avenging his father's death had to be taken. While he was still alive, a chance might arise again. It was terrifically unlikely, but it *might*. And so, even at the risk of betraying Parakka, he had to endure. Besides, anything he might use to end his own life had been removed from his person, and he doubted he had the willpower to smash his skull against the wall.

Footsteps. He looked up at the cell door. Not the boy and the Guardsmen, this time. The footfalls were more frequent and varied.

The time had come.

The mask of a Guardsman filled the wind-holes in the cell door. "Get on your knees, prisoner, for the Princess," he barked.

Ryushi smiled weakly. "Tell your Princess that if I get on my knees I may not have the strength to get up again," he replied, his voice full of scorn.

There was the sliding of a bolt and the door was pushed open angrily. Two Guardsmen came in, dragging him roughly up from the bench and shoving him to his knees. He did not have the strength to resist physically, but he could still defy them.

"You could cut off my feet and then I'd *have* to kneel," he said. "But I still wouldn't mean it."

The blow around the back of his head made his vision whirl. He squeezed his eyes shut to steady himself. When he opened them again, the Princess Aurin stood before him, flanked by one of her Jachyra and another aide.

"Get out, you two," she said to the guards with a hint of disgust in her tone. They obeyed, bowing as they left and closing the door behind them, sliding the bolt home after.

Ryushi stayed where he was, looking at her. She was breathtakingly beautiful, as the reports had said, thin and willowy with porcelain features and pale skin. Her hair was blacker than onyx in comparison, and her narrow frame was draped in an elegant gown of cobalt blue and white, with three turquoise stones on a pair of silver chains strung across her collarbone. For a few moments, there was silence as each appraised the other. Then Ryushi got up, struggling to his feet. The aide on Aurin's left made to push him back down again, but Aurin stopped him.

"There's no need for all this unpleasantness about kneeling and bowing, Corm. It's really only for the benefit of my subjects, yes?" She turned her steady gaze on Ryushi. "And you don't seem to think of yourself as such."

"You're very observant, Princess," he said, sitting down on the smooth creamstone bench again. He glanced at her other companion, the Jachyra. The same one he had fought in the Ley Warren, and who had come to his rescue in Takami's court. This one appeared to be Aurin's favourite.

"Forgive me," she said, following his eyes. "This is Tatterdemalion, Chief of the Jachyra. And this is Corm, a representative of the Machinists' Guild."

That was no surprise to Ryushi. The Machinists he had met that worked for Parakka were all instantly recognizable by their Augmentations, and this one was no different. The long black coat and high, rigid collar that covered the lower half of his face probably hid most of them, but the evidence of machine-flesh fusion was visible elsewhere on his body too. One hand had been replaced by a mechanical claw, with two strong pincers for his fingers and an opposing one for his thumb. Clustered around the wrist were all manner of minuscule tools, ratchets, minute metal tendons and other devices. Judging by the bulge of his shoulder, the whole arm had been done as well. His face was spare and gaunt, with one cheek replaced by a dull, bronze-coloured plate. A circular band ran around his hairless head, covering and replacing both eyes and one ear with grotesque mechanical substitutes that chipped and chittered as they operated.

"My name is Ryushi, son of Banto and a traitor to the throne," Ryushi told them, as if they needed to know. "I'd offer you a seat, but as you can see…" he trailed off, indicating the bare room.

"*The* Ryushi," Aurin said, spuriously impressed. "It is my privilege to meet you, after all I've heard. I have to admit I was a little disappointed when I heard of your death during the Integration, but I should have known this day would come sometime. People like you have a habit of coming back from the grave, yes?"

"Only because you guys never bury us deep enough," Ryushi offered as a rejoinder.

"Yes, well, that's a failing of my father's, perhaps. But not of mine," she said casually, with a cold smile. "First, though, I believe you have something for me."

"What's that?"

"I'm sure you've figured it out by now."

"I assume you want information about Parakka, then?" He gave her a shrug. "I don't know exactly what you expect. I've been in the organization just over a year; that's not long enough for them to tell me anything sensitive."

"Oh, I'm sure you're just being modest," Aurin said chidingly. "After all, Tatterdemalion himself saw you recruiting for Parakka at Mon Tetsaa."

The Jachyra's eyepiece whirred out fractionally, focusing on Ryushi. He was crouched in his customary coiled stance, watching for the slightest movement from the prisoner. Ryushi had no doubt he would be cut down before he got half the distance to the Princess's sleek throat.

"I do the recruiting, that's true," he said slowly. "Most people who've heard of Parakka have heard of me and Kia. So we go to collect them, to put them at ease, let them meet some of the people they've been told about; and then we pass them on to the real recruiters, the ones who are part of the central organization." He gave her a sympathetic look. "You've not made much of a catch, I'm afraid. I don't know anything. Like when your father caught Ty." He paused, and then smiled. "You royal types really aren't very good at this, are you?"

"Enough lies," she snapped, the colour rising in her cheeks. She wasn't used to being mocked. "I have subjects that can rip the answers out of your mind, if necessary." Her voice quietened. "It will be far more unpleasant than simply telling me now. The location of Parakka's base."

"Chita, on the Iron Coast," he replied instantly.

"Another lie!" she hissed.

"On Tetsu Mountain? Jii Lan in the western provinces? Deepwater? Even if I told you, you wouldn't believe me, Princess. What can I—"

She slapped him, hard, across the face; and with her touch came something else, an undercurrent of force that brushed his soul and made him quail at the contact, a power cold and dark and brooding. . .

He forced down the sudden fear and looked up defiantly into the Princess's eyes, which flashed with haughty anger.

"You're very easy to wind up, Princess," he said, his voice low. "I'd expect a little more restraint from the ruler of Kirin Taq."

She laid a hand on Corm's arm to stay him; he looked as if he would lunge at the prisoner at any moment. Tatterdemalion merely watched Ryushi, his mechanical features incapable of expression. Ryushi's face smarted, but he could sense that he had won a victory. He didn't care about the pain his disrespect would bring him eventually. He needled her out of spite.

+++ **My lady** +++ Tatterdemalion spoke up suddenly. +++ **Will you have us bring the Scour?** +++

Aurin glared at Ryushi hotly. "Well?" she

demanded. "It is your choice. Spare yourself the pain."

"You think you can do something worse to me than slaughtering my family?" Ryushi said, and suddenly burst into hysterical, desperate laughter, a mixture of fear and amusement. "Really, please try. I'd be interested to see it."

Aurin's chest heaved in indignation, but this time she controlled the angry flush of her pale cheeks. "You will regret the request you have just made," she said, and with that Corm knocked on the cell door and it swung open. Aurin stalked out, followed by her aides. The Guardsmen were nowhere in sight. For a moment, Ryushi thought that they had actually left him to walk free.

Then the Scour stepped into the doorway, and the blood drained from his face.

It wore a loose, black cloak, belted at the waist, which swirled around its feet as it came. Its hands were held together in front of it, buried in its long sleeves. But its chalk-white face was unhooded, and there were no features there. Shallow indentations or slight lumps indicated where eyes, nose and mouth should have been, but the Scour possessed only a smooth skull of naked flesh, uninterrupted by the features by which humans recognized each other. There was something inexpressibly horrible about their absence. But not as horrible as the paralysis which suddenly gripped Ryushi, pinning his heart to his ribs and making his arms go limp. Strange, then, that he still had breath to scream as the Scour clamped its fingers around his face and began to tear and shred at his memories. . .

"Are you alright, Princess?" Corm enquired in a high, nasal voice.

"Of course I am," she snapped, striding along the corridors of Fane Aracq, heading back to her chambers. Tatterdemalion dogged their heels. Ryushi's howls were fading behind them, but they still caught a faint shriek from time to time.

"I hope that hurts as much as it sounds like it does," Aurin muttered bitterly.

Corm frowned. This kind of pettiness was unusual, and did not become the Princess.

+++ **You seem angry, my lady** +++ Tatterdemalion observed.

"That's because I *am*," she replied sharply.

+++ **Why?** +++ the Jachyra enquired. Corm had noticed before that Aurin and Tatterdemalion did not adhere to the rules of conduct that should exist between ruler and subject, but such forthright interrogation still made him flinch inwardly.

Aurin pulled up short in the middle of the corridor, turned on the creature as if to shout, and then seemed to deflate a little. "I don't know. Why am I like this? His taunts are laughably ineffective. Yet they affect *me*." She paused. "Perhaps he has been trained by a wordsmith to add barbs to his tongue, yes? I will be more careful." She turned and resumed her walk.

The Machinist watched her back with his mechanical eyes as she headed once more for her chambers. He had been an aide to the Princess for five years now, since she was thirteen winters by the calendar of his Dominion homeland. And now she had come of age, grown into womanhood; and he feared for her. She had been brought up as a Princess, accustomed to being obeyed by everyone, with a power at her hands that was enough to make even the bravest man nervous. Children played with her because they were forced to, and because they were afraid of her. She had missed the tough lessons that children inflict on each other to harden their skins for the tribulations they will face later in life. Nobody had dared to insult her or go against her whims.

But a girl who was used to her own way was not about to sit back and let everyone else do things for her. And now, with her father gone and her coming of age, she had involved herself more and more in matters that were previously left to her underlings, things that she was painfully ill-prepared for. The incident with Ryushi was only one example. He had tried to ask Tatterdemalion to explain this to her, to warn her against herself, but it was useless; a creature like that had only a very slippery grip on the finer emotions. Most of them had been numbed and deadened by the cruel experience of being Converted.

"Corm," she said suddenly, making him jump. "The Machinists' Guild. Where do they stand?"

She already knew the answer to that, but Corm

replied anyway. It was another facet of her immature personality; she needed constant reassurance that her plans were not straying.

"The Master Machinist issued a communiqué a few cycles ago, stating that all was well, Princess. The Guild is pleased with the trade that your father's subjugation of the Dominions has brought. War makes profit, both in the building of war machines and in repairing damaged items."

"But. . .?" Aurin prompted, eager to hear again any sign of dissent against her father.

Corm frowned for a moment. He understood the reasons behind his Princess's coldness where her father was concerned, but there were times when her disrespectful attitude – at least when out of his earshot – gave him cause for concern.

"But now that the war is over," he continued, "and the Dominions are under his control, there are fears in the Guild that the profit will dry up somewhat. This in itself is not a catastrophe, but the unrest it has provoked has fuelled the cause of those who are wary of your father. They believe he will not be content with trading and paying for the Guild's services when he can invade the Citadel and turn the Machinists into little more than slaves. For precedent, they cite both the subjugation of the Keriags and the more recent Integration, when the King was not content with his power over the Dominions until it was totally in his grip."

"They may rise against him, you think?" Aurin asked, sounding almost hopeful.

"There are not enough of the dissenters yet. However, there had been a steady trickle of Guild members who had left the Citadel and taken up with Parakka, before they relocated to Kirin Taq. We believe that some of the dissenting Machinists are now using their Guild privilege to cross over at the Ley Warrens and join the reformed organization over here."

"Interesting," she mused, and then they were at her chambers. She led them into her largest room, where her great mirror was fused with the creamstone wall, and where white glowstones lit up the graceful curves of the windowsills, benches and tables. Like herself, the room's appearance was elegant and understated, with only a few ornaments of exquisite beauty breaking the simplicity.

"Sit down, please," she said to Corm. She had learned long ago that it was not worth making the offer to Tatterdemalion; he didn't even sleep, let alone sit. Corm thanked her and sat on a wicker mat, his Augmented eyes following her above the high ridge of his stiff collar. She walked over to one of the wind-holes, looking out, as she often did, over the provinces beneath her. After a time, she turned away with an expression of faint disgust.

"Tatterdemalion," she said. The Jachyra raised itself a little from its crouch and looked at her attentively. "What news from the Jachyra?"

+++ **The search for the Parakkan base continues apace, my lady** +++ he said, the last words almost inaudible under a sudden squeal of feedback. +++ **We hoped to acquire Whist from Takami-kos, in case he had gleaned any clues from his time with Ryushi; but the boy was gone, and we were unable to catch him** +++

"Takami," Aurin said distastefully. "I admit, it was a stroke of genius to use Whist to lure the boy here, even though it was my idea to use Takami as bait. But if we had not had spies in his court to warn you, and Takami's lust for revenge had got the better of him. . ." She turned aside for a moment. "Losing an ear is less than he deserves. But I will leave him be for now." She looked sharply back at Tatterdemalion. "What else?"

+++ **Now that Parakka know that their presence has been revealed, they have abandoned their secrecy where Resonants are concerned. Previously, they did not dare shift to the Dominions because they would alert us if they did. Now they have nothing to lose by that, and Resonant activity has increased dramatically** +++

"Can we use it to pinpoint their location?" Aurin asked halfheartedly.

+++ **Parakka have always travelled far away from any sensitive locations before shifting, my lady, so as not to lead us to them. And some, particularly the little girl, are very good at covering their tracks** +++

"They're throwing out branches again," Aurin said. "Spores of their organization, in case we wipe them out here. Gathering information about what is happening in the Dominions, yes?"

+++ **It would seem probable** +++

"You have not told my father?"

+++ **The Jachyra are ever loyal to you. And the King relies on us for information of that kind. We shall not tell him, if you so desire** +++

Corm glanced between the two of them and felt the ever-present worry about his Princess gnaw at his insides once more. These dangerous power games she played were one day going to trip her up. Her father had indoctrinated the Guardsmen to be loyal to him, and he was their first concern, even those who served and protected the Princess. He had given the Keriags to his daughter in one of his many attempts to buy her love; but his gift was also a curse that she openly resented him for. So she had spent her time winning the Jachyra over to her side, knowing that they were the linchpin of her father's information network. Her job was not a hard one; after all, the Jachyra hated Macaan more than Parakka did.

It was a strange thing, that Macaan's most trusted force were also his bitterest enemies. But though they kept it carefully secret from him, each and every Jachyra desired his death more than anything. For he was the one who captured them; he was the one who had them Converted, turned from humans to the nightmarish scarecrows of rag and metal that they were. For the Jachyra were Resonants, heavily Augmented by the Machinists' Guild under Macaan's orders, made into lightning-fast killing machines to carry out his bidding. It was a curious side-effect of the process that the Jachyra lost their ability to shift between worlds at will; but they gained instead the power to use mirrors as portals. It had been suggested that the loss of half their human body meant they could only half-shift, into the world of reflections, and so they were forced to travel in that way; but nobody knew for sure.

If the Jachyra were ever to rise against Macaan, they would be a fearful enemy. But Macaan was too wary to create such a force without some means of controlling them. For the Jachyra, like Macaan's other top aides, were implanted with special stones beneath their rags, stones that were linked to the indigo trigger-stone set in Macaan's forehead. With a thought, Macaan could end what was left of their lives; and while this would be no great loss to many of them, still there was enough humanity inside them to keep them in line at the threat.

"And what do you think of the fears of the Machinists, Tatterdemalion?" Aurin asked. "Are they justified?"

+++ **Possibly, my lady. Though perhaps your father will remain content with possession of both Kirin Taq and the Dominions** +++

"I doubt it," she replied.

+++ **As do I, my lady** +++ Tatterdemalion said.

She turned away from the wind-hole and walked slowly across the room, talking as she went. "So *now* what?" she repeated. "What will he do now? You know he won't be able to stop *here*."

Tatterdemalion's reply was uneasy, even through the wheeps and distortion of his voice. +++ **Perhaps the Unclaimed Lands. There are stretches of the Dominions as yet unexplored. Your father still has no firm grip on the nomadic tribes of the steppes or the desert folk. And there is always Deepwater, and whatever lies beyond** +++

"But it's all worthless!" Aurin cried suddenly.

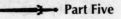

"And what good is it? What will he do with it? Give it to me? *I* don't want it! I don't even want *this*!" She swept a slender arm out towards the wind-hole and the lands beyond.

Tatterdemalion did not respond for a time; when he did, it was to change the subject. **+++ The Scour is one of the best, my lady. The prisoner should not be long in giving up his secrets +++**

"How long?" she asked.

+++ Ten cycles, if we intend to leave him the power of reason after we are done. Perhaps less, if we do not +++

"That's too long. If the Parakkans are sending Resonants about, we have to stop them before they can take root in the Dominions, yes?"

"Perhaps if you told your father, he could deal with it?" Corm suggested, but was silenced by a blazing glare from the Princess.

"*I* will deal with it. I will see the prisoner. Soon, in a few cycles' time. Let the Scour soften him up. Perhaps I can get out of him what we need."

+++ My lady, that could be unwise +++ Tatterdemalion ventured.

"At least let us use an interrogator, Princess," Corm pleaded.

"No. I will do it," she said, and the tone of finality in her voice told them that her will was firmly set in the foundations of stubbornness. She turned back to the window and rested her thin fingers on the sill. "Go now, both of you. I will send for you later."

+++ **My lady** +++

"Princess."

And then they were gone, the Jachyra through the mirror and Corm through the door, closing it softly behind him. Aurin stood alone and looked out over a land she cared nothing about, and listened to the silence for a time.

6

A Gesture of Support

"He's gone? What do you *mean* he's gone?"

"He's gone, that's all. He left to go off with Whist on some stupid point of honour to kill your brother," Calica replied.

"Why didn't you *stop* him?" Kia cried in disbelief.

"I *tried*," Calica shouted back. "Maybe if his sister hadn't been away on some fool mission to nowhere then *she* might have been able to."

"Don't try and blame this on *me*! You're the only one he listens to any more anyway!"

"And whose fault is that?"

"You're saying it's *mine*?"

"Of course it's *yours*! It wasn't me that cut him off from you. That was all your own work. If I—"

"*Please!*" the Convener roared, silencing them

both. The longhouse hushed, and the mutterings from the blackness outside the bright circle of wavering light faded. The firepit cracked noisily. Seated on their wicker mats around it, Kia and Calica glared at each other. Baki smirked at them, his ash-grey face creasing smugly.

"Enough of these petty arguments," the Convener spoke at last, his voice echoing through the room. "Why Ryushi went does not matter. The fact that he is gone and has not returned is sufficient. We have more pressing concerns at the moment; we cannot waste time speculating on what he may or may not be doing."

"Waste *time*?" Kia cried, but she was cut off by another voice.

"Your pardon, Convener, but what Ryushi is doing at the moment is of the very utmost importance."

It was Anaaca who spoke, a trim, middle-aged Kirin with long, free-falling red hair that contrasted sharply with her dark skin. She was the centre of Parakka's information network; a spy by trade and now a teacher of spies for the organization. She was regarded with some suspicion by the rest of the Council, but she was an invaluable resource and she knew it. Her narrow, cream-on-white eyes surveyed the Council before she continued.

"As you know, we have been trying for a long while now to get people into Fane Aracq for the purposes of gathering information on Aurin. It has proved so far impossible. However, we do have the next best thing; a spy in the court of almost every thane in Kirin Taq. Not necessarily in a position of any importance, but there nonetheless." She paused, smoothing her hair back over her head with both hands. "I have a page-boy in Takami-kos's court whose message reached me only today. The court is in uproar. Ryushi was captured there during an attempt to assassinate the thane, after which Takami-kos challenged him to single combat. The fight was stopped by Aurin's Jachyra. They took Ryushi with them, presumably to Fane Aracq."

"He's been *taken*?" Kia said, blanching.

"Your brother's recklessness has put us all in danger," she said, without a taint of emotion in her voice. "He knows far too much about

Parakka. Aurin will force his secrets out of him eventually. She may already have done so."

"Then what do you suggest, Anaaca?" the Convener asked, his eyes flickering to Kia as if expecting her to interrupt. She didn't, surprisingly; but only because Calica got there first.

"We get him out!" she said firmly. "We have to! For his sake and for ours." There was a mutter of agreement from those shadows seated outside the circle of firelight; they had not forgotten Ryushi's part in the destruction of the Ley Warren.

"We must get to him, that much is true," Anaaca said softly. "To divine how much he has told them, if anything. Get him out, if possible. If not, kill him."

"Kill him and I'll leave your *head* on his tomb!" Kia shouted at her.

Anaaca sighed. "I doubt that, girl. But all that is moot right now. First we have to get to him. A direct assault on Fane Aracq would be useless. Spies would take too long. We need—"

"You need *me*," came a voice from the darkness, and into the firelight stepped Gerdi, his impish face grave beneath the green shock of his hair. Kia subsided a little, settling back down.

"The Council recognizes Gerdi," said the Convener. "Speak."

"Look, spying's not my strong point and straight combat's hardly my brew," Gerdi said, looking at Anaaca. "And I'm no assassin, either. But I'm a Noman kid. I've got stealth in my blood. I can get into and out of anywhere, and you guys know it. Let me go, on my own. I'll bring him back somehow."

"He's just a child!" Baki protested, characteristically obstructive.

"I could be older than you think," said Gerdi in a dry, phlegmy voice; except that it wasn't Gerdi there any more, but an old and bent Kirin, tottering on a stout staff of warped wood. Those in the Council that did not know of Gerdi's talent exclaimed out loud in surprise, but those outside the firelight murmured in puzzlement. Only the Council had seen Gerdi change, for he could only influence the perceptions of so many people at one time. With the power of his Noman spirit-stones, he could make others see him as anything he chose; but the ability only worked on those he was able to direct it at, and though he was improving every day, he was still not strong enough to make a whole room full of people succumb to his illusion.

"You know he can do it!" Kia said. "I'll go with him."

"No, you won't," Gerdi said, his voice for once devoid of humour. "I'm gonna have a hard enough time as it is without you tagging along. If I go, I go alone." He addressed the whole of the Council. "I'm the best chance he's got. Let me do it."

"Those who agree?" the Convener asked. The decision was unanimous; even Baki put his hands flat in front of him in a gesture of support.

"Alright, you guys have got some sense," said Gerdi. "I'll see you when I get back." And with that, he walked out of the firelight and back into the shadows.

"Stay where you are, Kia," the Convener ordered, as she made to rise and follow. "He will do better without your interference. You can't help your brother, except by leaving the boy to do his job."

110

She hesitated a moment in indecision, her distress evident on her face, then got to her feet and plunged into the darkness after him.

"Uncle Hochi?" Elani asked, more to let him know she was there than out of any real doubt as to his identity. It was hard to mistake Hochi, even in the dim Kirin Taq light and with his back turned. He was at the edge of the artificial clearing at the top lip of the valley where Base Usido resided, a narrow strip of land where the forest had been pushed back to allow the sentries on the huge mechanical lift near by a chance to see and react to an attack from out of the forest. Shadowy metal skeletons stood about, bits of half-constructed machines and items waiting to be loaded on to the lift.

Hochi looked over his shoulder in alarm from where he was leaning against a thick stack of girders. "What are you doing out here? It's dangerous!"

"Gerdi told me where you'd gone," she replied. "He said you two had an argument and you went to cool off."

"And the lift sentries let you come up the canyon wall alone? They should know better. *You* should know better."

Elani's eyes fell to the ground. "You want me to go?" she asked, her voice hardly audible.

Hochi hesitated for a moment, then sighed and heaved himself down on to the grass. "Come and sit with me, Elani."

Her face shifted from doe-eyed sadness to sparkling joy in a single jump, and she scampered over to where he sat and threw herself down alongside him, nestling between him and the girders that rose at his flank.

"Whatcha looking at?" she asked eagerly.

Hochi pointed a meaty finger out into the forest. Sparks of light danced there, very distant, popping in and out of sight in the black depths of the forest.

"Oh," said Elani, her elation muted a little.

"The Banes are getting closer," Hochi said. "There's more and more of them every day. They're drawn by our spirit-stones."

"Why?" she asked.

"Nobody knows," he said simply.

"We'll be okay," said Elani, toying with her dress, the hem of which had become muddied. "It's happened loadsa times before. We can handle a few Snagglebacks and Snappers."

"I hope so," he replied. "You know that a young Kirin boy called Paani was actually *bitten* by a Bane yesterday?"

"I thought Banes didn't attack people," Elani said. "They just scavenge off dead bodies."

"Exactly. The boy just dropped into a coma. He doesn't respond to anything. Where the Bane that bit him went, we don't know either." He looked down at his hands. "These are bad days for us."

There was a pause for a time. "Are things alright with you and Gerdi?" she asked.

Hochi frowned, his bushy brows gathering like thunderheads over his small eyes. "That fool boy. He wants to get himself killed. No one's got into Fane Aracq before, let alone got out again."

"Kia says that might not be true; Aurin would have covered it up if it had happened, just like all the other things she—"

"Oh, of course, Kia *would* say that," Hochi

113

grumped. "She doesn't care about Gerdi. She's only worried about her brother."

"And what about you, Uncle Hochi? Do you care about Ryushi?"

"Obviously I do," Hochi said, sounding a little uneasy at admitting such a thing. "He's Banto's son, for one."

"Don't you owe it to Banto to look after—"

"Curse it, girl!" he snapped. "Letting Gerdi get killed is not going to help Ryushi one bit!"

Elani fell silent, looking at her lap. She knew how Hochi felt about the Noman boy. Despite their antagonistic relationship, the boy was practically a son to him.

"I can't stop him, anyway," Hochi said, his voice diminishing in volume. "He's always gone his own way."

"Kia wanted to go with him," Elani commented, picking out a strand of her fine black hair and chewing on it absently.

"She's upset about Ryushi," Hochi said. "She knows she couldn't do any good, but she wants to do something. Gerdi will slip away from her if necessary, but I'm sure she'll see sense before that."

"I'm surprised Calica didn't want to go too."

"What's she got to do with anything?" Hochi asked, looking down at the little girl who sat in his shadow.

Elani blinked back at him in surprise. "Don't you know? Calica and Ryushi are in love."

"Mauni's Eyes, Elani!" Hochi exclaimed. "You can't just go around saying things like that!"

"Why not?" she shrugged. "It's true. Just look at them."

"I haven't noticed anything like that," Hochi said firmly. "It's just your imagination."

"If you say so, Uncle Hochi. Not that you *would* notice, anyway, with all the mooning you've been doing over that pendant of yours."

"You know how important this pendant is to me, Elani," he replied gravely.

"Yeah, I know," she replied, wrapping her arms round her knees and looking up at the curling corona of light that was the Kirin Taq sun. Unlike Gar Jenna, Base Usido had no need for canopies to protect itself from being seen by aerial reconnaissance. There were wild wyverns here, and worse things that plied the skies above

115

the shattered landscape. The Princess's wyvern patrols were few and far between in this dangerous place, and those that went in were as likely as not to never come out again. The Parakkans had lost many mounts and riders before establishing the safest routes to fly, avoiding the feeding-areas and brood sites of the winged Rift beasts; and they had lost more men and women in their difficult task of domesticating the wild wyverns than nested near Base Usido. Wyverns, unlike most creatures, were found in both Kirin Taq and the Dominions; it had been suggested that breeding pairs had been brought over by Resonants far back in history, but nobody knew for sure. Like everything since the Integration, it had been a hard and costly struggle; and now that it seemed to be finally paying off, it looked like they would have to run again.

"I had. . ." Hochi began suddenly, and then stopped.

Elani nudged his leg. "What?" she prompted.

"I had hoped for an answer," he said downheartedly.

"An answer for what? From the pendant, you mean?" she asked.

"Broken Sky," he said, confusion and frustration written on his face. "What does *that* signify? All this time I spent trying to puzzle over what Tochaa meant when he gave me this thing" – here he touched the small silver medallion that rested beneath his shirt – "and when I'm told what it is, it raises more questions than solutions."

"Why don't you ask Iriqi?" Elani suggested. "He might know."

"He's gone off somewhere with Jaan. The Council are voting whether to let him into Base Usido or not." He frowned. "*Division with the eventual hope of unity,*" he said, repeating the Koth Macquai's words to him. "What does it mean? Tochaa asked me to bring Parakka to his people, and I've tried to *do* that; I've worked myself to the bone over this last year to help make Parakka a force in Kirin Taq. But this? I don't know. How can I know what he meant?"

"You can't," Elani replied. "You just have to make your best guess."

Her sudden switches from childishness to maturity did not faze Hochi in the least any more, but still he found that he could not be satisfied with her answer. "If the Sundering that the Kirins speak of is the division," he mused. "Maybe the bringing together of the worlds is the unity? But Macaan's already *done* that with the Integration. It doesn't make any *sense*."

"Uncle Hochi, I'm worried about you," Elani said. "You've got to stop thinking about it. Remember what the philosopher Muachi said? Sometimes answers are like sleep; the harder you look for them, the better they hide."

"I wish I *could* stop, Elani," Hochi said, a great sigh making his back swell. "I wish I could."

Calica rode the great enclosed plain outside Base Usido, her thoughts studded by the rhythm of her pakpak's feet on the grass. She knew about the increase in Bane activity, and the threat it posed to the settlement, but it was not enough to stop her. She had to get out and alone for a while, to organize herself. Away from the constant industry of the Base, and the endless calls on her attention. Just

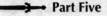

herself, and the wind rushing past her as the pakpak
sped across the great expanses of blank grass
between the soaring cliffs that hemmed her in.

The Council meeting had gone on to other
things after Kia had left, but she had scarcely been
able to bring herself to concentrate on them. Her
thoughts had been full of Ryushi, and the danger
he was in. She had wanted to run with Kia, to see
what she could do, full of the vain hope that she
could possibly help in some way; but she had
restrained herself. She tried to tell herself that the
decision was nothing to do with pride; because
any reaction on her part would have revealed to
all who were watching how deeply she felt for
him. It didn't work.

And so had passed the rest of the time in the
lone circle of light. The decision to let Iriqi into
the settlement had been made, and a messenger
sent to Hochi to tell him to find the creature and
its perpetual companion Jaan. Reports were made
on some of the forays into Dominion territories,
mostly involving Elani. There was little that they
had learned that was not already known by other
channels; Macaan had subjugated the greater part

of the Dominions, crushing utterly any resistance against him, and was using his now-stable foothold to implement the same kind of measures that were used in Kirin Taq to ensure that the downtrodden people never got up again. But it was early days yet, and hope still existed that the operation would bear greater fruit.

She had been unable to focus on the meeting. On top of all her confusion and worry about Ryushi, there was something else on her mind. Ever since she had first touched Macaan's earring, way back before the Integration, she had been having sporadic dreams of the Princess. There was no theme or linking subject to them; they were as random as her dreams usually were. But they all had the common bond of featuring Princess Aurin somewhere, and when she awoke she was often convinced they had been real for a time. She told herself that this was a side-effect of entering Macaan's memories, for the cruel King had a fierce and hopeless love for his daughter that was powerful enough to invade her own mind. But as time passed, the dreams had increased in both frequency and potency, and now she was not sure any more. She could not help remembering the familiarity she had felt when she had first seen the grown Aurin in Macaan's memory, something more than just recognition. It troubled her.

Recently, the dreams visited her almost every other night.

"Calica!"

At first, she thought she had imagined her name being called. It was a faint sound, and seemed to come from a long distance away, flitting past her ears.

"Calica!"

This time she did hear it, and she turned her face into the swirling stream of her orange-gold hair to look behind her. There, catching up with her fast on a pakpak of her own, was Kia.

There had been plenty for Kia to think about on the return journey from the Unclaimed Lands. At first, she had only been obsessed with how she had failed the test, let them all down, that her character was not strong enough for the Koth Taraan to trust. But her self-blame only lasted for so long, and it soon gave way to other thoughts. Ty had worried about her, for she had barely spoken since she had emerged from the settlement and given them the news that they were returning, empty-handed but for a single one of the Koth Taraan. She had hardly noticed. She had been intent on picking apart the events that she had seen in her dream-visions while in the pool, on analysing the things the Koth Macquai had dredged out of her.

Insights that even you yourself may not be aware of. Premonitions. Dreams. Hopes and fears. The pool strips you to nothing, human child, and leaves only that which cannot be washed away: the truth.

The surreal events that she had been part of during the test had begun to take on a semblance of meaning as she fought to put them together. The most difficult thing was being honest with herself, allowing herself to believe the answers that she came up with. But as she began to accept the things that she had seen, she became more and more convinced that they carried with them a truth free of all self-deception.

Takami's truth was the easiest. She had faced him on a pinnacle of rock and beaten him, but all that had seemed automatic and predetermined. She only gained the power of choice when it came to the simple decision: let him die, or let him live. She remembered how all the evil he had committed had flashed through her mind at that moment, and yet still she reached out for his hand.

Why had he been missing an ear?

She hated him. That was unavoidable. But she had sometimes wondered, in the same way her twin had, why her hate for him was not as strong as Ryushi's. Why *her* fury was reserved for Macaan and his troops.

But in her vision, Takami had been corrupted by the shadow. It wasn't his fault. And in the most hidden depths of her heart, Kia believed their brother could be saved. He had killed their father, but he was just a pawn. Macaan was the real evil. Macaan, the shadow.

Did she really believe that? On the surface, no. It was Takami's choice to betray them, Takami's initiative to sacrifice his family for his own gain.

123

But somehow, down in a place where logic and reason were powerless, she did believe. She held in that darkness a tiny flame of hope that would not allow her to despise her brother utterly; and much as she wanted to put that flame out, she could do nothing about it.

Then there were other signs, clear indications of emotions that she would not have previously admitted to herself. The shadow had stolen Ryushi away from her, and it had hurt her terribly; just as the conflict that they had been thrown into was tearing them apart now. The shadow had killed her mother, just as in real life she had died for Parakka, fighting against Macaan.

Macaan. Macaan. It all came back to him. He was the root, the cause, the wellspring of all the strife that Kia had endured since being ripped out of her home and cast adrift in an unfamiliar world. He had said he was her father, and he was right. Because of him, she had been reborn; the carefree, happy girl that had lived on Osaka Stud had become a warrior, an outlaw, even a leader. When Macaan's troops had destroyed her home, the old Kia had been destroyed with it. A new Kia had emerged, one better equipped to deal with the tribulations of her new environment. But she had lost so much in the transition. . .

The Koth Macquai had been right. Her interests were purely selfish. She had wanted to get the Koth Taraan on their side so Parakka could survive and eventually win, but underlying it was all one single ambition; to see Macaan dead. If she could somehow plug the fountain of discord that he represented, her ruined life might return to what it was. Maybe she could find real peace again, her and Ty. Maybe.

But there had been someone else in her visions. Calica. And Kia needed to have words with her about that. About the truth.

Calica reined in her pakpak and Kia brought her mount to a halt alongside. She waited a moment for Kia to catch her breath after the exhilaration of the ride, studying her with naked suspicion in her eyes. Kia shook out her hair over her face and retied it into a ponytail, then met Calica's gaze as if only just noticing she was there.

"Well?" Calica asked. She was not giving any

ground; Kia was the one who had been cold to her for over a year now, and if the girl was here for a reconciliation, she was not interested.

"I need to talk with you," Kia said, glancing around across the plains in a habitual check for approaching Rift beasts.

"I'm not going anywhere. Talk."

Kia frowned slightly at Calica's hostile tone. She should have expected it, really, but it still made her own tone turn aggressive in response.

"I told you and the Council about the test I had to take for the Koth Taraan," she said. "What I didn't say was that some of it concerned you."

"Oh?" Calica queried.

"I wanted to clear some things up, y'know? Make sense of the visions I had, what they meant and so on."

"I'll help you if I can," Calica replied, her words dripping with distaste. There was a moment's pause.

"So what's the connection between you and Aurin?" Kia asked, and Calica was not quick enough to keep the surprise off her face. "I see that there *is* one," Kia commented flatly.

"There's no connection," Calica protested. "What are you talking about?"

"I saw you twice in the visions. Each time you were with Aurin, dressed the same or holding hands or something. More like twins than me and Ryushi are."

"That's not much of a stretch," Calica shot back acidly. "You're hardly even like brother and sister any more."

"Don't change the subject."

"Well, what do you want me to say?" she cried, and her pakpak crabstepped nervously at the tension in her voice. She roughly pulled it back into line. "You had a dream. So what? You think because you dreamed something that it's real? You think just 'cause some creature tells you that you'll experience insights and truth that you actually *will*? You're looking too hard, you wanted this Koth Taraan thing too much. You wanted too much to be *right*. You're not being objective, Kia. That's—"

"My mother *died* because of you!" Kia shouted suddenly. "Is that objective enough for you?"

The speech froze in Calica's throat, her mouth

half-open. Shock and sorrow battled in her eyes, but she was unable to tear them from Kia's steady green stare. A cold fire burned there, frost and steel. Calica's lip trembled for a moment as she fought to find words in her lungs, but her body betrayed her and she could not make a noise.

"I heard them talking about it," Kia said, her voice like a wolf slinking up on its prey. "The day before they left. I was asleep then, but somewhere in my mind I must have been awake, because the visions took me back and let me listen. You sent her to her death. There was an ambush, a trap set, and you didn't warn them."

"I didn't *know*!" Calica choked, finally forcing her tongue over the dam of her shock. "It was a little village west of Tusami City. It should have been simple; just a meeting with a few farmers who wanted to know more. I don't know what happened. Maybe one of their own sold them out. But there were Jachyra waiting for them when they got there. How Banto got away . . . I don't know that either. Your mother, though. . ." she trailed off. "She never got out."

128

"They trusted you. It was your information. Your fault."

"I couldn't have *known*!"

"My mother's blood is on your hands," Kia said. "And in case you need reminding, she was *Ryushi's* mother also." She wheeled her pakpak, the sudden upswell of emotion making her want to get away from Calica before it overtook her completely. "If he makes it back from Fane Aracq, I'll be sure he knows just who was responsible."

"Kia!" Calica cried, turning her own beast to follow as Kia sped away. "Kia, no!"

But her protest was cut off by a sound, a sudden wail that split the valley and chilled her blood. The alarm siren. A glance around the cliffs confirmed that all the lifts were being hastily drawn down, that all the Parakkans outside of the protection of Base Usido were rapidly making for sanctuary. She urged her pakpak forward and it sprang to her command, racing after Kia, back towards the settlement.

Base Usido was under attack.

7

Far From Over

Awareness was becoming an increasingly unwelcome state of mind for Ryushi, but it had a nasty way of forcing itself upon him from time to time, reminding him that outside the sweet peace of sleep and unconsciousness there was a world of pain waiting for him. It had been eight cycles now, perhaps, though he really had no idea any more. He had been starved for that long, given only the barest of subsistence rations. He had been visited by the Scour many times. His head simultaneously ached and felt numb, like a cramp in his brain. His joints throbbed, his stomach felt full of knives, and it hurt to move his eyes too much.

He felt like he wanted to die.

But this time, when consciousness roughly

mugged him and dragged him back into reality once more, he found that he was not alone in his cell. Curled up on the floor as he was, his eyes opened to see a long white boot in front of him. He did not need to look up to see who it belonged to. Instead, he gritted his teeth and pushed himself into a sitting position. He wasn't yet so weak that he couldn't straighten his back to face his enemies.

Aurin sat on the smooth creamstone bench that protruded from the wall of the cell, her slender legs draped in a simple white-and-jade dress, her hands folded in her lap. She looked immaculate in contrast to his dishevelled appearance, and her narrow, curved eyes watched him closely as he arranged himself. How long had she been there, watching him sleep? He felt somehow violated, that he had been so defenceless before her.

"I took your bench; I hope you don't mind," she said. "You didn't seem to be using it."

Ryushi ran a hand muzzily through the short, fat tentacles of his hair and looked at her blandly. "My cell is your cell, Princess," he said.

A tiny smile tugged at the edge of her mouth.

"How true. I'm told you put up quite a fight against the Scour."

"If I ask you for some water first, would you be offended?" he asked sarcastically.

"Of course not. You must think me an ungracious host." She called for a guard, and a pitcher of water was brought in for him. He took a drink, and the water was painfully unsatisfying in his stomach. He looked wearily up at the Princess.

"I'll die before you get what you want," he said. "There's nothing in my mind for your leech to find, Princess. I told you, I am not as much a part of Parakka as you think."

"Then why do you torture yourself so?" Aurin asked, leaning back a little, the looped braids at the side of her head swaying with the movement. "Stop fighting the Scour. Once we've established what you don't know, it will be over."

"And then you'll kill me," Ryushi said with a grim smile. "Sorry, but I'm not keen to hasten that particular outcome. You tell your Scour I've got a lot of fight in me yet."

"Yes, I can tell," said Aurin sarcastically,

running a critical eye over his sunken face and weary body.

Ryushi felt his shoulders begin to sag forward, and pulled himself back straight again. He was more weakened by lack of food than he had first thought. "You're very brave, Princess," he said, more to distract her from his plight than out of any real desire to talk. "After all, you've no bodyguards here now. What if I should attack you? You could be dead before the guard gets through the cell door."

Aurin laughed lightly. "I think you'll find I'm perfectly capable of defending myself, yes?" She raised a hand, and it seemed to seethe with a dark green and black radiance, like a heat-haze around her skin. Ryushi felt himself go cold as he recognized the power he had felt when Aurin had slapped him in anger. She met his eyes and said: "I can kill you with a touch. And without your spirit-stones to help you, you are little more than another peasant warrior. Do not be foolish." She closed her hand, and the shimmering disappeared.

"So," Ryushi said, fighting to ignore the all-consuming ache in his body. "To what do I owe the honour of this royal visit?"

"Must you keep up this scornful politeness, Ryushi?" Aurin said with a sigh. "It is becoming tiresome."

"Would you prefer I insulted you outright?" he asked. "Forgive me, Princess, but this is as civil as I get towards those who starve and torture me."

Aurin waved a hand, dismissing the point. "Let us talk of other things, then."

"What did you have in mind?"

"I want to know about you," she said. When he gave her a curious look, she added: "Call it an attempt to understand the mind of my enemy."

"A trade, then," Ryushi said, taking another sip of water from the pitcher. "A question for a question." He met her dark eyes. "It's only fair."

"I could simply Scour the answers out of you," she said.

Ryushi shrugged. "It's your choice, of course."

She did not reply for a moment. Then she laughed to herself and said: "Very well, Ryushi. A question for a question."

"You know, of course, that I won't answer anything you might ask me about—"

"Oh, no. This is of a purely personal nature."

Ryushi coughed, a little noise that rapidly grew into a loud hacking. When it had subsided, he glanced wryly at the Princess and said: "Anything you learn about me will have a very short-lived value."

Aurin ignored the comment. "Tell me, then. What is the attraction of Parakka to the people? What was the attraction for you?"

"You really need to ask?" Ryushi said; but by the expression on her face at his words, he saw she genuinely meant it. "Okay. I guess I have nothing to lose by honesty, so I hope you're ready to listen to the truth." She leaned a little closer, indicating that he had her full attention.

"Parakka is an attraction because it's an alternative to you," he said, watching her face for a reaction but seeing that she kept her thoughts well hidden. "Your ancestors had ruled Kirin Taq for generations, keeping the land in relative peace and order, before your father decided that being a custodian of the land and its people was not good enough for him. A King should do well by his people; Macaan didn't want that. He simply crushed them. Ruling by fear takes all the effort out of being a King, because nobody dares stand up to you; but once you start, you can't ever stop. Because people hate to be afraid, and under the fear there is always that hate. You're like your father. You rule by fear. And if you ever stop, the people will rise up against you in revenge for what you've done to them." He paused, taking a drink of water. Aurin did not say a word. He took it as a sign to continue.

"Parakka is about freedom. It's about elected leaders, and each person having a voice with which to influence the whole organization. It's where a person makes their own choices and gains their own position based on their merits, not on age, race, sex or birthright. It's where a farmer and a Machinist are equal, and nobody is turned away until they have proven themselves unable to adapt to our credos. It's not perfect by a long way, but we make it work." He looked deep into Aurin's eyes. "Can you understand what something like that means to a person? To suddenly have a measure of freedom again, instead of feeling like cattle to be herded by your Guardsmen and your Keriags, under threat of death from your whims and edicts? To have a choice, however small, in the shaping of their future and their *children*'s future?" He held her gaze for a moment, seeing nothing there, and then broke off. "You don't, do you? To you, a person is not a person. It's a subject, a pawn, to be used or disposed of with no more thought than a stick. You've put yourself so far above the common folk for so long, that they're as insignificant as ants to you."

There was a silence then, during which Aurin appeared to study him closely. "Are you trying to anger me again?" she said at last, though her voice sounded as far from anger as it was possible to be.

"That's two questions, Princess. It's my turn."

She settled back on the bench. "Ask, then."

"How do you feel when you command a whole village to be executed?" he said levelly. "To have the Keriags overrun it, and have them butcher the men, women and children with their *gaer bolga*? Do you ever put yourself in their place, think how they must feel as they see their families slaughtered before them, the pain as they meet their end?"

"I think you have already answered your own question, yes?" she replied. "They're as insignificant as ants. You have already made up your mind about me, it seems."

"Forgive me, Princess, but you hardly deserve any sympathy from me," Ryushi said. "Still, that's beside the point. What I think doesn't matter. I want you to tell me how *you* feel. Is it really nothing at all? Or do all those deaths weigh on your conscience at night?"

"At night?" she said with a faint laugh. "Your Dominion habits have not left you yet, I see."

"You're avoiding the question."

"I don't wish to answer it."

Ryushi shrugged again. "Then the game is over. Goodbye, Princess. You can send your Scour if you want any more information from me." He lay back down on the floor, turning his back on her, and pillowed his head with the crook of his elbow. After a few moments, he closed his eyes.

Several minutes later, his breathing deepened as his exhausted body drifted irresistibly back towards sleep.

She sat there watching him, for a long while, her head full of uncomfortable thoughts. Later, when she knocked on the door to be released, she ordered a page-boy to fetch bedding and a good meal for the prisoner.

Getting into the palace was easy for Gerdi. It was Festide; the nobles had gathered, and a great market was going on inside. The tall, white, oval gates of the tradesmen's entrance were always open, and a constant stream of traffic poured in and out of it, bringing wares to sell or livestock for the kitchens. Disguised as a Kirin, he walked beneath the huge creamstone arches and into Fane Aracq, tagging himself on to a caravan and following them in. In the crowded market hall, with a little make-up, concealing clothes, and just a touch of his spirit-stone magic to perfect the illusion, he passed himself off as a Kirin quite well. It was only a tiny use of his power, but he had to maintain it for many people at once, and it exhausted him. A necessary drain, though, for his Dominion eyes would make him stand out a mile and probably get him arrested.

After that, it got a little trickier. Fane Aracq was divided into many sections, and getting from one to another was an extremely difficult process. The first major problem was getting out of the market hall and into the corridors of the palace. There was only one access route, and it was for palace personnel only, not farmers or traders. Anyone entering or exiting the antechamber at the end of the short corridor that ran off the market hall was checked visually, and each guard had a private password known only to themselves and the Gatekeeper. It was not as simple as walking in wearing a Guardsman's uniform – not that he would have fitted in one anyway. All Guardsmen had to remove their helmets, and the Gatekeeper had a pin-sharp memory for faces and knew exactly who was supposed to be there and who was not. He was a tall, dark-haired Dominion man with pale skin and a pinched face, who dressed in robes of black silk. It seemed that Dominion-folk in the nobility's employ were tolerated; after all, some of the nobles like Takami were from the Dominions themselves.

Gerdi had learned of these primary security measures by posing as an ignorant Kirin cereal-thresher, and walking up the hall after a couple of Guardsmen. After observing the checks that were carried out on them in the small, arched antechamber inside the gate, he made up some blather about how he was here to see his cousin. The Gatekeeper asked him for his password. He had none, and was firmly told to leave. He was lucky; they believed that his character was really muddled enough to walk into Fane Aracq and think he could get into its heart, and they suspected nothing more.

That first run had been tiring. Having to maintain his illusion for so many eyes at once – for there were other guards besides the Gatekeeper – drained him quickly. Next he tried something simpler – posing as a Guardsman when one of the palace folk left to travel by pakpak to a nearby town. He hailed the rider down, a cook-boy, under the pretence of searching for a spy, and then tried to extract the boy's password as proof that he was allowed in the palace. The boy was initially intimidated by the tall, black-armoured figure that Gerdi presented him with, but when Gerdi got on to the subject of passwords he became immediately suspicious, and Gerdi ended up changing his story and telling the boy that it was a security test to be sure that nobody would give up their password to a stranger. Bemused and uncertain, the boy left with a worried expression on his face, and Gerdi was still at a loss as to how to get into the palace. All other entrances, like the land-train depot and the entrance for nobility, were guarded even more fiercely than the tradesmen's one. And all the while, he thought of Ryushi, trapped in there, maybe being tortured at the orders of the Princess. . .

In the end, he took a gamble, and it paid off.

A way back up the road that the land-trains ploughed along was a large inn, used as a rest-stop for the traders and farmers. It was also where some of the Guardsmen went on their time off. Gerdi spent several cycles hanging about that place before he managed to get into a conversation with a suitable Guardsman, for they were not frequent visitors, and they were suspicious of those who tried to befriend them. It was vaguely disconcerting to meet a Guardsman out of his black carapace of armour; somehow, he had never really thought of them as being human underneath. But this was a Dominion man, blond-haired and a little gruff, and Gerdi almost enjoyed his rough anecdotes and heavy humour. Once they got talking, he was careful not even to approach the subject of passwords or the palace; he merely concentrated on memorizing every detail of his face, his speech, his mannerisms, and learning everything he could about the man. What he found was that the Guardsman was on a ten-cycle leave, and was going away to see his parents in Dacqii. Perfect.

While he and the Guardsman talked, Gerdi spun a fabric of lies about his own past, all the while trying to maintain the faint illusion that kept the make-up on his face and hands looking good enough to fool onlookers. He was wearing a cowled cloak and they sat in a dim, sheltered corner; but even so, he soon had to make his excuses and leave, for his stones were being drained almost dry by their constant usage.

After resting once more, and armed with his new knowledge, he tried the Gatekeeper again. He still had no password. But he did have a plan.

There had been quite a commotion when the Guardsman that Gerdi had been talking to at the inn came stumbling into the antechamber, his helmet missing, clutching a bleeding wound on his forehead.

"Let me through!" he said, in his bluff and rugged voice. "I need a healer!"

"Jutar!" one of Guardsmen on sentry duty cried. "What happened? I thought you—"

"My pakpak threw me," Jutar replied, followed by a string of epithets directed at the animal. "You know how I hate those things."

"Aye, and it makes me wonder why you choose to ride one after—"

"I was bringing it as a present for Mother's birthday," he interrupted. That was easy for them to swallow; they knew how Jutar doted on his mother, and it *was* her birthday soon. "Now let me pass, I need to have this looked at."

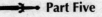

"Your password," said the Gatekeeper, standing up in his sheltered booth at the side of the antechamber. Each person who passed through had to whisper it to the sallow man before they could proceed.

"For Cetra's sake," said one of the other Guardsmen. "You know who he is. Let him pass."

"Your password," the Gatekeeper demanded again.

"Fridia? Kenia? Reto?" Jutar said, waving his hands as he listed off the names of members of his family. "I can't think! I can't remember! My head is hurting! Let me through!"

"His wits have been muddled by the blow to his head," one of the Guardsmen, obviously not a friend of Jutar's, pointed out with no small amount of glee.

"I need a healer!" Jutar cried again, his legs buckling suddenly. He staggered forward, and only just managed to bear himself up again.

"Use your eyes, man!" the first Guardsman shouted at the Gatekeeper. "He needs to—"

"You may pass, Jutar," said the Gatekeeper, waving him away with sudden disinterest.

"Do you want someone to go with you?" another of the Guardsmen enquired as Jutar stumbled past them and out of the antechamber.

"And have you leave your posts?" he said as he was leaving. "No. Stay and guard the Princess's palace. What would she say if you let an intruder get past you?"

The Gatekeeper looked sharply after him as he left, but Gerdi hadn't been able to resist his last cheeky comment. His plan had worked, and he was in. But it was far from over.

8

A Species Indigenous

In the isolated world of the Rifts, chaos had erupted. All over the valley, the Parakkan troops swarmed from their outposts back towards the relative safety of Base Usido, running for their lives. The air resounded and echoed with the shrieking *yip! yip!* of the Snagglebacks, a strangled sound half-bird and half-dog which stabbed at them from the depths of the foliage. On the ridges of the valley walls, the trees were bright with the luminescence of Banes as they flowed sinuously between the trunks, writhing and coiling as they led the other Rift-beasts towards their prey. The great mechanical haulage-lifts had long been lowered down the sheer cliffs, but everyone knew this would not slow the creatures by much. They had faced attacks like this before several times now; it was part and parcel of living in the Rifts. They knew that their only hope of survival was to get behind the Base defences.

Kia and Calica were racing across the plains as the noisy mass burst out of the treeline and came boiling over the edge of the cliff. The Snappers scuttled head-first down the rock walls as if they were spindly yellow spiders, their ridged tails curling behind them for balance. Kia felt a shiver of repulsion as she remembered the overlapping jaws and milk-white eyes of the creatures that had terrorized them on Os Dakar. Meanwhile, the Snagglebacks took a slower route down, their immensely powerful fingers crunching into the stone to provide them with handholds as they descended. The Banes swirled around them, shadowing them like eager lapdogs.

Kia's eyes hardened as she saw them beginning to pour down into the valley. They had appeared on both sides at almost the same time, and suddenly the rim of the cliffs was alive with a churning, thrashing mass of creatures that tumbled and crawled down towards the plain like a foaming tide. In their haste, the occasional creature was swept off the edge by the weight of numbers behind it and sent flailing to its death, hundreds of feet below.

"Looks like the whole of the Rifts have come out to play," Calica said from behind her. "*Ride!*"

They spurred their pakpaks to fresh vigour, and their mounts responded to the urgency in their riders. Ahead of them, the spiked outer wall of Base Usido rose out of the plain, a vast, jagged semicircle against the cliffs. And from behind it, with a screech, three enormous wyverns suddenly tore upwards, their vast double-paired wings spreading as the momentum of their skyward leap began to dwindle. Kia's eyes ran over their thick, squat bodies, the white plates of bony armour that covered their black hides, the long necks and twin tails; and then they dipped in their flight and began to streak across the plains towards her and Calica, the riders on their backs hunched low. They were carrying force-cannons, mounted on specially modified harnesses, and Parakkan Artillerists rode shotgun to operate them.

Kia and Calica instinctively ducked as the creatures flew low over them, pushing a blast of wind in their wake which buffeted their faces as they passed. They turned around to look over their shoulders as the wyverns wheeled into a shallow turn, and the Artillerists let fly with their force-bolts, blasting pulses of invisible energy into the attacking creatures, blowing them off the cliffs as they scuttled or crawled down them.

"Kia! The gates!" Calica yelled, and somehow Kia heard her. She looked ahead, already knowing what had to be happening. The huge metal gates were being closed. The Base security dared not wait any longer. They were being locked out. Even at this distance, she could hear the screech of the mechanism as the two halves of the gate began to slide together on its heavy rollers. She gauged how fast they were going and how far they had to go to reach the Base.

No dice. They'd never make it.

She exchanged a glance with Calica, who was riding alongside her. It conveyed nothing. They had been too long at odds to share the

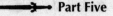

kind of communication she had with Ryushi. So she turned back to the gate, gripped the reins of the pakpak hard in one hand, kept it steady on its course towards the Base, and closed her eyes.

"There's still two riders out there!" one of the Base security cried, squinting through a Kirin spyglass with his cream-on-white eyes from his vantage point atop the perimeter wall.

"The Snappers are reaching the valley floor! There's nothing we can do!" shouted another Kirin, his superior, from ground level.

"It's Kia and Calica! We can't leave them outside!"

"We've got no choice. If the Snappers get to the gate before it closes, all these defences won't be worth a thing!"

"We can stop the gates. They'll make it!"

From where he stood at the lever to drive the grinding, clanking gate mechanism, another Kirin shouted to the ranking security member on ground level over the din. "Do we keep closing or not?"

"Keep closing!" came the reply, as he waved his hand to indicate he should continue. "We can't risk it. They'll have to take their—"

He was drowned out by a great rumbling and tearing of earth, and he staggered back a step as the ground between the two closing halves of the gate suddenly spasmed and retched out an arm, an enormous, thick forelimb composed of the dirt and stone of the plains. It slammed down, its fat, unwieldy fingers digging in as if something was climbing up from beneath, and then it pulled itself out. Slow, massive, the golem broke the surface of the ground and hefted its huge body upright, a creature knitted from the very soil it came from. As the fissure it had risen out of closed beneath it, it planted its spatulate feet wide, and braced its hands and shoulders against the closing gates of Base Usido, then opened its ragged mouth in a roar as it took the immense strain. The gates shrieked and ground to a halt, propped apart by the golem's arms. It swept the shallow pits of its blind eyes over the assembled security men.

THE GATE STAYS OPEN, it said in a deep

rumble, the rattle of stones in its throat rendering the words only barely decipherable.

To that, the Base security had no reply.

Peliqua arrived at the main gate at almost the same time as Calica and Kia came through it, riding full pelt on their pakpaks, ducking beneath the legs of the behemoth that held the gates open for them. Calica had the reins of Kia's mount in her hand, leading it for her while her concentration was fixed on maintaining the golem. No sooner were they through than the golem collapsed in a shower of dirt, the security personnel set the machinery in operation again and the gates powered onward, pushing the debris of the discarded golem aside as they rumbled closed. Kia's green eyes flicked open as Calica pulled both their mounts to a halt, and they jumped from their saddles to the grass.

"Thanks," she said to Calica, her voice a little dull from the weariness that she had sustained from maintaining the golem.

"You'd have been too slow otherwise," Calica

said. "I led your pakpak. You kept the gates open. We're even."

"This changes nothing, you realize," Kia said.

"I know."

Peliqua ran up to them, her red braided hair curling in the torchlight around her grey-skinned shoulders as she stopped.

"Oh! Oh! Are you two alright?" she asked.

"I will be when I find out who it was who tried to close that gate on us," Kia said, her eyes ranging the assembled security personnel, who were all racing to secure the perimeter of the Base against the approaching swarm. As if to emphasize her point, the gates slammed shut behind her.

"There's no time for that now," Calica said. "We were cutting it close anyway; it was a judgement call, and whoever did it was overcautious."

"I'll give them overcautious," Kia growled. "I'll—"

"*Drop* it, Kia," Calica said firmly.

"What are you talking about?" Peliqua put in, then changed her mind with her customary flightiness. "Oh, it doesn't matter. Have either of you seen Jaan?"

"Jaan? He's with that Koth Taraan thing, surely," Calica replied, glancing around as if impatient to be somewhere else.

"Yes, but *where*? He was outside the compound last I heard. I'm so worried!"

Calica looked back at her. "We sent Hochi to tell him that Iriqi would be allowed into the compound with him. Hochi will know."

Peliqua's face broke into a sudden smile. "Thanks, Calica. I'll go find him." With that, she sprinted off towards the clusters of huts where their living-quarters were.

"I'm going to check the clifftop defences," Calica said. "You coming?"

Kia met her eyes blandly, then they flickered away. Running across the settlement towards them was Ty. "I've got my own concerns," she said.

For a moment, they just gazed at each other, the long history of their antagonism and the aftertaste of their recent conflict running between them. Then Calica turned away and ran after

Peliqua, towards where Base Usido backed up against the cliffside. Kia watched her go for a moment, then turned and went her own way. Each of them had their priorities to follow in a crisis, she reflected, as Ty came up to her with words of relief and greeting. Except that one of hers was even now languishing in Aurin's grip.

On the plain, the battle continued in earnest. The Rift-beasts darted between the force-bolts that pounded them from the Parakkan wyverns, heading towards the rough semicircle of Base Usido. They were suffering heavy losses, for the airborne defenders had multiplied fourfold by now and they had no way to strike back at the winged creatures or their riders; but they went on, heedless, driven by the Banes towards the island of prey that was the Parakkan stronghold. The thin, wiry forms of the Snappers jostled with the massive shoulders and corded muscle of the Snagglebacks as they stampeded across the blue grass, grey under the cold eye of the Kirin Taq sun.

"What are they doing?" Ty asked. "This is

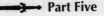

suicide for them. I don't know about the Snagglebacks, but Snappers are brighter than this."

Kia tilted her head in agreement, her face shadowed in the twilight. The Snappers that she had fought on Os Dakar had been a devious and cunning breed, and Ty had spent a lot longer there than she had. "It's the Banes," she said at last. "They're doing this. They've got some sort of plan."

"Plan?" Ty asked, incredulous. "They can't *plan*."

"No?" she replied. "Did you notice that they started coming down opposite sides of the plain at almost exactly the same time? From two points that were a mile or more apart? Don't you remember when they destroyed that outpost of one of the collectives to the East, when they pulled an ambush on them? That takes forward planning. No one knows *what* Banes are capable of. Hardly anyone has seen them in action."

They waited on the defensive ledge that ran below the lip of the perimeter wall, where warriors could stand to repel anything that somehow managed to scale the forest of bladed spikes. The ragged attackers were almost upon them now, the air full of the Snagglebacks' *yip! yip!* cry, and though there seemed to be no apparent way for the creatures to get inside the compound, they were running full pelt at it as if they could batter through by sheer weight of numbers.

They couldn't, Kia thought. *Could they?*

All eyes were turned outward. The camp was in a state of frantic preparation. That was why nobody was in the medical hut to look after the patients, whose unconscious forms were wrapped in blankets underneath the orange glowstone radiance. And that was why nobody noticed when a young Kirin boy called Paani suddenly opened his eyes, awakening from his coma without the slightest evidence of disorientation, and got out of his bed. He stood up, wearing only his long undergarments of coarse wool, his chin-length red hair falling uncombed around the ashen skin of his face; and then he walked to the door of the hut and opened it.

The boy knew more of the Banes than Kia could hope to guess at. As he walked through the camp, people running past him and shouting in all directions, nobody gave him more than a second glance. If the fact that he was half-dressed seemed unusual, it was not enough to stop anyone to ask him why; if he did not walk with his usual light skip but with a fast, purposeful tread today, then it was a difference so slight that only his mother or his friends might notice. But his veins ran with fire now, scorched with energy, and the brain that drove his body had a new occupant.

The Banes were creatures of pure Flow – the rushing energy that ran beneath the earth in torrents called ley lines. The ley lines behaved in many ways like the rivers they were often likened to. They branched and divided, curved and twisted; they had small tributary channels which leaked out into the surrounding ground. The Rifts, due to its heavily sunken and broken terrain, ran very close to one particularly strong example of these, the planet's arteries. And the excess energy that bled out of the earth formed the Banes;

congealed clots of the very essence of the planet. Their arcane nature granted them a kind of strange intelligence, but it also cursed them with a hunger, so that they were drawn like moths to flame when the Flow was in use. Mostly they sated themselves on the recently dead, the release of life-energy as their essences rejoined the Flow from which they had come. But with the arrival of the Dominion-folk, they had found a new source of energy: spirit-stones, gorged with Flow. And all collected here, at Base Usido.

The Parakkans thought that the Snagglebacks and Snappers followed the Banes for some reason. They were wrong. The creatures were pack animals, and the Banes simply possessed their leaders, and led the rest like a herd. Once it had bitten, a Bane could dissipate itself into the bloodstream of its victim, the particles of the Flow that composed its body taking over the weaker ions that ran through its prey's veins. By manipulating the electric impulses in the brain in a similar way, a Bane could gain control of its victim's body. As it had with Paani.

Now the young Kirin boy walked through the

milling defenders towards the main gate. Everyone's eyes were turned outward, watching the approaching stampede, wondering why they were running to impale themselves on the vicious spikes of the perimeter wall. Only one man stood to guard the mechanism that operated the main gate. Paani strode confidently up to him, meeting his puzzled gaze with a friendly smile.

"Hey, kid, you shouldn't be—" the guard began, but Paani clamped a hand on his forearm and there was a short crack of Flow energy. The guard's joints buckled and he slumped to the ground, his life extinguished. The boy stepped over the limp corpse, to where a long, slightly rusted metal lever was buried in a mass of huge cogs and gears. Paani did not have the strength to pull it alone, but he gripped the handle anyway. The Bane in control of his body dumped adrenalin into his system, a sudden surge that boosted the strength in his muscles tenfold. He pulled the lever.

The Banes' previous attacks on Base Usido had been tests, probing the defences, working out the best way in. They had been small affairs, conducted while the main gathering of Rift-beasts was being carried out. This was the real thing.

The lever moved.

The Bane left Paani's body in a fizz of tiny lights as the boy's heart gave out under the massive overdose of adrenalin he had received.

The gates began to open.

Ty felt a flood of ice spread through his chest as he heard the grinding and clanking of the gates start up. His eyes were still on the approaching mass of Snappers, Snagglebacks and Banes, but his ears gave him in a split-second a premonition of what was about to happen.

Plan? They can't plan!

He heard his own words of a few moments ago, echoing hollowly. They could plan, alright. Parakka had underestimated them. And that was going to cost them dear.

"Close the *gate*!" someone shouted, an edge of panic to their voice.

Ty saw a pair of men leap down from the ledge on the inside of the wall, half scrambling and half sliding down the ladders in an attempt to get to the mechanism in time. Two other security men on the ground floor were doing the same, running across the short stretch of grass as the two metal halves of the gate withdrew to their fullest extent.

But it was hopeless. The Banes' timing had been impeccable. They had allowed no margin for mistakes. At almost the exact second that the gates finally came to a rest, the stampede hit Base Usido, and the attackers exploded into the settlement. They caught up with one of the guards a hand's breadth away from the lever, sweeping him into their ranks and tearing him apart; the others that had made the run to mend the breach suffered the same end. The Parakkans' one chance at sealing the gates and keeping the enemy out was buried under the heaving mass of bodies as they surged into the Base, and the carnage began.

"Get down there! Keep them out!" Kia cried over the sickening crunch and slice as hundreds of their attackers, propelled by the weight of numbers behind them, threw themselves on the jagged spikes of the perimeter walls.

But some of the enemy were already clambering up the ladders to the wide ledge while the rest of them dispersed across the compound, and the defenders turned their attention inward to deal with the new threat. A wyvern screeched overhead, the Artillerist on its back sowing force-bolts into the horde, the blast of its wings blowing Kia's hair about as she stood with her bo staff ready. Ty stood by her side with his hooking-flail spinning.

It was a Snaggleback that finally gained the ledge in front of them, reaching around one sentry's careless sword-swing to grab his arm and fling him bodily to the ground below. It pulled itself up to their level and began loping across towards them, as they prepared to receive its charge.

The Snagglebacks were a species indigenous to the Rifts, where their vicious nature and hardy constitution made them the ideal predator for the environment. If they could have been said to resemble anything, it would be a huge, hairless ape. Their skin was a grey-brown hide sewn thick with veins that bulged over limbs and a torso crammed with muscle; their hands and feet were massively strong. They had no eyes, only the wide nostrils of a snout; but it was their jaws that were the most disturbing thing about their appearance. When not in use, they were sheathed in the flesh of their cheeks and chin, only the tips of their crooked, long teeth visible between their lips. But when they opened their mouths to feed or bite or make their shrieking *yip! yip!* cry, their jaws pushed outwards, their lips skinning back all the way along them to reveal the stringy flesh of their gums and the roots of their fangs.

Now Kia and Ty faced one of them as it ran along the ledge towards them, its bunched muscles pistoning as it came. Kia lashed at its head with her staff, cracking it around the skull and making it skid to a halt, checking its headlong charge. Ty used the moment of disorientation to send his hooking-flail slicing out, the three bladed balls carving three different paths of blood along its back. It made a strange, low mewling sound of pain, then swung one heavy arm at Ty; but he was too quick, and had pulled himself away. The ledge was wide, but not so wide that a creature as big and cumbersome as the Snaggleback could fight comfortably on it, so Kia took advantage of the clumsy overswing and levered her staff behind its knee, shoving it further off-balance and buckling its legs. It tipped over the edge with a shriek and fell into the stampede below, knocking some of its kindred to the ground where they were trampled.

"Go for the lever!" Ty cried over the tumult, but it was useless. Everybody was engaged in the fighting. There was no way anybody could close the gate while the creatures were still pouring through it; and no way to stop the creatures except by closing the gate. A no-win situation. Unless. . .

He turned suddenly to Kia, his eyes alight with inspiration. "Kia! Use the earth! Seal the gate!"

It took a moment for his words to sink in, but then her own face changed into a grim expression of agreement.

"I'll watch you," he said, laying a hand on her shoulder as a pair of Snappers that had fought their way along the ledge came scuttling towards him, their lean, yellowish bodies and overlapping fangs picked out in the torchlight of the camp.

She closed her eyes, trusting him totally.

Gripping her fist, she called out the Flow. Her spirit-stones began to sear as they released their energy, pouring into the ground, agitating the soil, meshing the particles, knitting them under her will, until…

The ground at the entrance of Base Usido began to churn for the second time that day, but this time it was no golem that came forth. It was a wall of earth and rock, as solid as any metal barrier could be, that burst out from beneath the enemy's feet and shot upward, flinging them away. In a moment, the gap that the gate had left was filled with the thick earthen barricade, flattened at the top into a narrow platform. The creatures on the outside pulled up short, some of them being crushed into the unyielding surface and slumping to the ground; but the pause was only momentary, for the barricade did not have spikes like the perimeter wall did, and they began clambering up it.

Kia began to falter. The golem, and now the wall of earth she had raised, had tired her out; she did not have the strength to repel the creatures that were scaling her wall.

"Get to the breach and hold it!" Ty yelled, his hooking-flail smashing through the skull of a Snapper, sending it flailing over the wall and on to the spikes on the outward side. Most of the troops, seeing the chance that had been presented to them, had already run to do just that, and the fighting atop Kia's barricade became savage as the defenders fought to repel the invaders and keep them from getting any more of their number in. Others concentrated on driving away those creatures that sought to get up to the ledge and attack from behind those who protected the wall; but the enemy's numbers were thinning rapidly now as they split up and ran through the Base, in search of easier prey.

Outside, the stampede had stopped. Kia noticed this as she returned to herself, having no need to maintain her barricade any more now that it was set and hardened. The creatures were no longer throwing themselves on the spikes, but concentrating on trying to clamber over the corpses of their dead to get inside through the heavily guarded gate. The wyvern-riders and Artillerists swooped over them again and again, each force-bolt blast pulverizing more and more of the enemy as they ran about in the open.

Kia managed a weak smile amid a lull in the fray. They had sealed the breach, and they were holding the enemy out on this side. Just.

But what of those that had got inside?

9

Trickery And Wordplay

If asked, Aurin would have been unable to say how she knew when her father was in his sanctum. Similarly, Macaan could not determine exactly how he knew when his daughter would be calling, and made sure he was there. The process operated on a kind of instinctive level; or perhaps it was something to do with the mirrors themselves, for their glass had been impregnated with fine grains of powdered spirit-stone residue, and who could say what subtle side-effects that would have?

So it was that when Aurin stood before the huge mirror in her chambers and willed it, her reflection faded into the reflection of her father, standing in his sanctum, surrounded by flashing blue ripples from the glowstone-bowls of water that flanked him. He looked the same as he always did, flawlessly handsome and straight-backed, his piercing eyes of the lightest blue gazing steadily from beneath his cascade of pure white hair and the small indigo stone in the centre of his forehead. He wore a long cloak of white over a black velvet robe, belted with an ornate gold clasp.

"Daughter," he said, his voice quiet yet crystal clear. "How goes it in Kirin Taq?"

"The same as always, father," she replied curtly. "Little changes in this realm with the passing of the cycles, yes? A small incident here and there. I have dealt with them."

"Good. Things are settling here in the Dominions. Perhaps soon you will be able to come over and join me for a time."

Aurin's face turned to false sorrow. "I'm afraid that I will be too tied up with the affairs of court to leave Kirin Taq for a while. It will soon be Festide, and the nobles of my provinces will want me here. Who else would they grovel to otherwise?"

A hint of amusement passed over the King. "You should be thankful for the mundane. It seems that our fears of Parakka resurrecting itself were unfounded."

"Did you ever really take them seriously, father?" Aurin asked. "Parakka are dead and gone. Worrying about them is a waste of time."

The conversation faltered. Aurin gazed at her father coolly, her silence more eloquent than speech. Macaan seemed about to say something, took a breath to give the words voice . . . and then changed his mind. Still Aurin stood like a statue. They were not father and daughter; just strangers trying to fake their roles. Perhaps she seemed cold to him only because she was unwilling to play out the deception. Well, let him struggle for sentences if he wished. His child had been reared in the care of nannies while an absent father conquered lands to thrust into the arms of his little girl. It was his choice to maintain the fiction, and his fault that he did not know his part well enough.

"I will be in contact again soon," he said at last, indicating that he had given up attempting to bridge the impassable chasm to his daughter for now. "I am going away for a short time, to survey the southern deserts here. There is still a little . . . resistance there."

"Till then," Aurin said, and the reflection wavered and shifted back to her own.

She had no compunction about lying to her father. It only galled her that she had to lie at all. Not that lying bothered her much; it was just that it seemed to be beneath her. A Princess should not have to lie. She watched herself in the mirror for a time, flattering her vanity, until the sound of hasty footsteps outside her door brought her round.

"Come in, Corm," she said loudly, and the Machinist stepped through the smooth, arched doorway, his eyes a frenzy of tiny clicks and chatters as they adjusted to the different light in the room. Even with the high collar of his greatcoat hiding his lower face, Aurin could tell that he was agitated.

"Speak," she said. She had tried to discourage her closest retainers from sticking to protocol, but it had never taken with Corm. She knew he would stand there in silence indefinitely until she bade him to report whatever was troubling him.

"Princess, I have just spoken with the jailor," he said, his voice even higher and sharper than usual. "He tells me that the Scour has been called off the prisoner, that it was a direct command from you. Surely he is mistaken, Princess?"

"Really? And why is that?"

"Because it would be –" Corm began, then swiftly and wisely checked himself. "Because such an act would make no sense," he finished.

Aurin turned his back on him, looking out of one of the wind-holes with her hands linked loosely behind her. "There was no mistake. I did order that we stop using the Scour."

"But Princess!" Corm protested. "It . . . just. . . *Why*?"

"The Scour is too rough a method to get what we want from him," she said. "We might find the location of Parakka, but we'd lose a lot of precious information in the meantime, yes?" She looked at him over her shoulder, her narrow eyes blinking laconically. "You know what happens to people if we Scour too hard. Some die before they have the chance to give up what we need. Ryushi is our only link to Parakka at the moment;

if he dies, we lose everything. We have to be careful."

"But you said yourself that finding Parakka was of the utmost urgency," Corm said, visibly fighting to keep the frustration out of his voice.

"And I have changed my mind," she said implacably. "I have spoken with the prisoner several times now. I am learning from him, Corm. He tells me things about the attitude of the people I rule over that I have been unaware of. He tells me about the low folk, and what they think of me. He talks to me about the common people's lives, and how they are affected by what we do, and—"

"These are *lies*, Princess!" Corm cried. "He is taking you in with lies and trying to prolong his own miserable life."

Aurin turned back to the window, a dark and menacing glint in her eyes. "You forget yourself, Corm. Don't ever interrupt me again."

"I . . . apologize, Princess," he said, bowing his hairless head; but the way he flexed the metal grips of his Augmented hand showed that he was just as angry as he was chastened.

"The point is this," she said. "It is to my advantage to fully realize the potential for rebellion in my kingdom. That way I am better equipped to deal with it, yes? Having the Scour tear out the location of Parakka's base may well kill him, but it is much more likely to scar him enough so that he would scarcely be capable of continuing to educate me."

Corm was silent. Her explanation sounded rehearsed; she'd obviously justified it over and over to herself. But who was she trying to convince? After all, she'd never felt she had to explain her actions to an underling before.

"My Princess, may I speak freely?" he said at length.

Aurin waved a hand to indicate that he should proceed.

"Please understand that what I say comes only from concern for yourself, and that I am more than willing to accept any punishment you see fit to deal me if I should offend you by saying it," he explained. "But your attachment to this prisoner is a most unwise development, Princess. You are not trained or experienced enough to deal with him, and he has snared you with his trickery and wordplay. He has duped you into calling off the Scour, and I understand that you have also abandoned the starvation tactic. He is less a prisoner now and more of a guest. You may think this is your idea, Princess, but I assure you it is—"

"Don't treat me like a child, Corm!" she snapped, her posture suddenly alive with indignation. "I am not some little girl to be deceived by the words of a stranger. I have come of age, I am a woman now! The prisoner does not have the wit for your *trickery and wordplay*; it is *I* who is manipulating *him*! Each privilege I allow him makes him trust me further. And with each breath, he gives away more and more about the attitudes and priorities of Parakka. The more we know of the enemy, the easier they will be to predict, yes? A few cycles will make no difference to us; Parakka are scarcely a force we need to fear with the Keriags on our side. When I have learned all I can from him, then you may Scour him until his brain melts if you wish; but until then, do *not* presume to treat me like a fledgling."

Her words rang around the chamber, dying quickly into a throbbing silence. Corm's head was bowed inside his tall collar, the bald dome of his skull pale in the white glowstone-light.

"Besides," Aurin said, a little calmer but still acid-tongued, "what do you think is going to happen, Corm? I'm hardly going to let him escape, and he's not likely to persuade me into giving up my throne, now is he? Where's the harm that you can see? I'm listening and learning. He isn't *brainwashing* me, as you seem to think, yes?"

"Forgive me, Princess," he said; and this time he sounded like he meant it.

"You're forgiven," she snapped. "Get out."

Corm bowed further, this time from the waist, and retreated hastily through the archway, closing the ivory door behind him. The moment he was out of her sight, he dropped his façade of an apology, and his face set hard in the island of flesh between the brassy metal of his cheek and the mechanical band around his eyes and ear. He walked away down the cornerless, creamstone innards of Fane Aracq, frustration lending speed to his heavy steps.

What did she think she was doing? *What?* Before, when Macaan was here, a whim as dangerous as this would never have been tolerated; he was the only one who could check her. But she was too used to her own way, and in her flush of independence she was indulging herself far too much. She was too stubborn to listen to reason.

Treat her like a fledgling? How ironic, that she could not be dealt with like a child but that she could act like one.

Ryushi paced his cell. His strength had largely returned to him over the last few days, and the aches and pains in his body had gone. He had a hard cushion on the bench to sleep on now, and he had been furnished with regular meals that, while not exactly fine fare, were nourishing enough.

What he could not fathom was why.

Having nothing else to do and no human contact other than Aurin's visits and the page-boy's food deliveries, he spent his time thinking. Thinking of what had gone wrong, thinking of how stupid and foolish he'd been, thinking of his sister, of Calica . . . and of Aurin.

She plagued his mind now, and no matter how much he tried to steer it towards something else, it always returned to her. Her image superceded any other in his head. He couldn't understand her. It was by her orders that his torture had stopped, she had made that clear enough by hints and asides in their conversations; but she would never tell him why she had done it.

She fascinated him. She was so easy to anger, and she would leave the cell each time in a high rage at a barbed comment or an observation that he made; yet each time she would return a little later and the sparring would begin again. Some of the time she seemed almost unaware that he was a prisoner at her behest, and spoke to him like an equal, expecting him to do the same. He invariably disappointed her. It was a bizarre situation; she knew that Ryushi was part of an organization dedicated to her downfall, yet sometimes she treated him almost as a friend. There was always the haughtiness, the temper, the condescension bubbling just under the surface, breaking out at the slightest provocation, but she was *trying*.

Why?

They talked of many things, of events in Kirin Taq, of the circumstances of her father's conquest and the opinions of the varying sides, of the lives and trades of villagers in the various provinces in comparison to those of the Dominions. They speculated on the mystery of the Deliverers, and talked about the Machinists, and sometimes even exchanged stories about childhood. Usually Aurin was reluctant to speak on matters of any personal importance, but when she refused, Ryushi would always clam up like he had the first time. Then she would storm away, and come back a little later ready to talk about it. And despite the fact that he had not wholly abandoned his snide tone with her, she would often reward him for a particularly lengthy conversation. He would be given a meal from her kitchens instead of prison food, or a cup of wine; once he was escorted out of his cell and allowed to bathe while his clothes were washed.

"You aren't afraid of me, are you?" she asked once. It wasn't a question, it was an observation.

"How could I be afraid of you? What can you do to me that's worse than you've done already?" he had replied.

"It wasn't me that had your family killed," she said, her voice going cold.

"But how many of me are out there?" he had asked, his eyes flat and grey. "How many who *have* had their families killed by your order?" He had paused then, and sighed. "The whos and wherefores of responsibility don't matter. You, Takami, Macaan; you're all part of the same thing. And you'll all pay the same price."

He had seen her react then in a way she had never done before; she looked shocked, and hurt, as if someone she trusted had suddenly turned and plunged a knife into her belly. Then she had got up and silently left.

Aurin was an enigma. Why did she obsess him so? At first, it had been because he had finally come face to face with his enemy, an enemy that so few people had ever seen and less had survived to speak of. Aurin, like Macaan, had been simply faceless forces up until now, the anonymous power behind the Guardsmen,

Keriags and Jachyra that they fought. But now, he had a face to link it with.

And it *was* a beautiful face. She was staggeringly attractive. Perhaps this, too, contributed to the way he felt about her. There was no denying that she had a physical magnetism that was far and above anything he had felt before; but she was his sworn enemy, and he knew that beneath the surface lurked a mind that was much less beautiful.

Now, though, he told himself that it was curiosity that made him think of her almost constantly. Why, why, why? What was her scheme? Why was she acting so irrationally; or was it just that he could not see the plan she was carrying out, that she was being too devious for him to follow?

He had been pacing for a long time when the bolt drew back and Aurin was allowed in, banishing the guard out of earshot. He was surprised to find that he greeted her with a smile. . .

What is happening to Ryushi? Surely he can't
have forgotten that Aurin's a cold-hearted tyrant,
with blood on her hands?
He's not falling in *love* . . . is he?

There's only one way to find out. . .

Read

Part Six

Can love *really* conquer all?

Remember these classic Broken Sky moments?

Ryushi blasting the golem. . .
"Okay," he said quietly. "Enough."

The first appearance of a Jachyra. . .
*The stranger's fingers spread wide, and with a
sudden shrik, sharp metal nails appeared.*

The Deliverer performing a pah'nu'kah. . .
*Deliverers were shrouded in mystery,
surrounded by legend.*

The arrival of Elani. . .
*"I want you to look after her. She's a very
special girl."*

Tatterdemalion reporting back to the King. . .
"A few Resonants still elude us."

Calica fearing for the future. . .
*"Macaan is building up to something.
Something terrible."*

Hochi paying Gerdi back for stealing the pastries. . .
"I'll make a pastry from your head!"

**You won't if you haven't read Parts 1–4.
How can you bear it?**